THE MARINE'S MARRIAGE

Fuller Family in Brush Creek Romance, Book 1

LIZ ISAACSON

AEJ
CREATIVE WORKS

ISBN-13: 979-8612753223

"But I would strengthen you with my mouth, and the moving of my lips should assuage your grief."

—JOB 16:5

CHAPTER 1

When Wren Fuller pushed into the office she ran to the shrill sound of the phone ringing. Already. She sighed, this Monday shaping up to achieve the horrible reputation all Mondays dealt with.

She'd arrived at A Jack of All Trades, the family owned and operated business, fifteen minutes early. Whoever was calling could leave a message. Wren dropped her purse at the desk where she sat and continued through the door to the left so she could put her lunch in the fridge.

It would be nothing short of a miracle if her sisters came in today. They sometimes did after their house-cleaning jobs, but Wren had them pretty well booked today, much to Fabi's disgust. The oldest of the twins, Fabi loved sleeping in as much as the rest of the Fuller clan, Wren included.

But whatever. Wren tucked her hair behind her ear

and deposited her brown bag in the fridge. She paused and looked in the mirror to the side of the door that led back to the reception area, trying to make her blonde hair grow longer just by staring at it.

It was in this weird, in-between stage she hated. But she didn't like her hair long either, so she'd cut it. But she didn't have a feminine enough face for a short, pixie cut, so she was growing it back out.

No matter what she did, her hair seemed determined to make her life more difficult.

As she settled into the ergonomic office chair she'd insisted Daddy buy, the phone rang again. Though they still didn't open for another ten minutes, she answered the call with a chirpy, "A Jack of All Trades, it should be a good Monday," and waited for a chuckle or at least half a giggle.

She got silence.

"Hello?" she asked.

"Yes, hello," a man said, his tone the no-nonsense clipped kind. "I need a maid."

"Well, we certainly can help you with that." Wren's four sisters managed to keep their schedules full with the amount of dust and dishes that the townspeople in Brush Creek wanted someone else to take care of. Especially in the summer, when they'd rather go camping, fishing, hiking, or strawberry-picking.

"Let's see," she said, tapping to wake her computer. Sometimes it took an extra few seconds to find the WiFi after being asleep overnight. Thankfully, it fired right up today, and she had the family's online calendar open in less time than it took to inhale and exhale.

"I can get someone out to you next Tuesday."

"Next Tuesday?"

"That's right. It's best if you get on our regular schedule. That way, we'll come at the same time every week, or every two weeks, or once a month. It's—"

"I just need someone once. I can clean my own house."

"Oh." Wren blinked, the man's tone the type that shut down conversations and left no room for argument. "Then I can get you an appointment for next Tuesday." And if he could clean his own house, why had he called her and asked for a maid?

"I need someone today. Is that possible?" He removed the demand from his question. Sort of.

"I'm sorry," she said. "My girls are all on other jobs."

"I just arrived in town," he said. "I just need help for a few hours today, and then I can get my stuff moved in."

"Oh, you're new?" Wren leaned back in the chair and put her shoes on the edge of the desk. "How did you hear about us?" Wren wasn't sure, but she could've sworn he growled.

"Erin at the bakery. And Landon up at the horse farm."

Wren grinned and nodded, though this new stranger to Brush Creek couldn't see her. She pushed the glasses she didn't need to wear higher on her nose. "Some of our best clients."

"I've got to take Octagon up to the horse farm, actually. Then I'd like to move in."

"So you want someone to come right now, this morning?"

"If possible. I'll pay double the rate."

"You don't even know what the rate is." Wren enjoyed this exchange more than she should've. She should tell this guy to find someone else and begin her morning Solitaire game until she had to get some work done for the day.

"Can you send someone or not?"

Wren could send someone...herself. Technically, she could be out of the office for the morning. Any calls that came here would forward to her cell, and she could pocket the extra cash as a tip.

"Give me a few seconds to check with one of my girls." She put the man on hold as he started to protest, a grin flirting with her lips. She wasn't exactly dressed for scrubbing sinks or mopping floors, but she could do it. Heaven knew she'd spent enough time growing up cleaning everything from tack rooms, to trucks, to toilets.

Still, she loved this shirt with the bright purple My Little Pony on it. Bleach would not be kind to it, so she resolved to grab an apron from the closet in the kitchen before she went out on the job.

She pressed the hold button and said, "I can send Wren."

"Great," he said, almost a deadpan.

"Where am I sending her?"

"I'm on Traverse Road?" He spoke the name like a question, but that wasn't the reason Wren's blood turned cold.

"Traverse Road?" she repeated it like a question.

"Yeah. It's the first one after you turn. I guess a family named Hammond used to live here."

"I know it," Wren said, the rundown house flashing through her mind. She straightened, intending to tell him she was Wren and she'd be there in twenty minutes.

"Great. Good-bye." He hung up before Wren could say anything. She tilted her head and stared at the receiver, wondering if the entire call had been a prank. It didn't seem to be. She hung up and exhaled as she stood.

"Good news, Wren," she said. "You can change before you go *next door* and clean the house that should've been knocked down years ago."

WREN HADN'T SEEN ANYONE AROUND THE OLD Hammond place, ever. Her house sat a hundred yards past it, on the same side of the street, and she drove by every morning and every evening. So really, anyone could've come and gone during the day and she wouldn't have known.

She liked to think she would've noticed tire tracks, or something left on the porch, or that one of the fence slats had been nudged slightly out of place. But she hadn't noticed anything.

After she changed and pulled into the driveway, she still didn't see anything that told her someone had purchased this home and planned to live here.

Because it was pure madness. The porch needed to be replaced, as did the railing, the roof, and all the windows. The whole thing needed to be remodeled, and Wren actually worried that her foot would bust through the steps as she climbed them to the front door.

So she'd put on a few pounds. She didn't care. She'd listened to her mom put her value in the number on the scale, and she didn't want her life to be measured in pounds. Maybe she chose nachos when she should've opted for the Caesar salad. But at least she could walk around with a smile on her face.

"Hello?" she called when she noticed the front door gaped open a couple of inches. No one responded, and she caught sight of a scrap of paper taped to the doorframe.

Come on in and get started. I took my horse up to the ranch. Be back later.

Relief rushed through Wren, and she pushed the front door open further. The inside of the house hadn't fared much better than the outside, much to Wren's disappointment. He hadn't given specific instructions for what he wanted cleaned, but it was obvious the kitchen in the back needed a thorough scrub from top to bottom. All the floors needed to be stripped of their dust. And one peek down the hallway showed three bedrooms and a bathroom that all needed a vacuum, a duster, and a whole lot of elbow grease to make them habitable.

"Did he even look at this place before he bought it?" she wondered as she set her bucket of cleaning supplies on the tile in the kitchen. If he had, he would've known he couldn't just move right in.

She started in the kitchen, glad when clear water came from the sink. Wren didn't worry about splashing on the floor, as she'd clean that last.

Two hours—and at least a bucketful of sweat—later, Wren finished the kitchen and living room. She'd emptied her vacuum three times, but the carpet was walkable now. The walls had been wiped down. The light fixtures and shelves had been relieved of their cobwebs. All cupboards and appliances had been scrubbed, and the floor glinted where the sunlight hit it through the back windows. She'd abandoned the bulky black frames she wore to make herself look smarter long ago, as it was too hard to keep pushing them into place as she worked.

She smiled at her progress and wondered when the man would return. It certainly couldn't take that long to drive a horse up to a ranch and drop him off. She moved into the bathroom, secretly hoping he wouldn't return until she was finished. She could bill him.

Bent over the tub, she heard the distinct sound of boots entering the house.

"Hello?" a man called, and he sounded softer, kinder, than he had on the phone.

Wren scraped her bangs off her forehead, cursing her hair for the tenth time that morning as it stuck to the back of her neck. It wasn't quite long enough to pull into a ponytail, and she had the fleeting thought that she'd like to shave every last hair from her head.

She hadn't even made it to her feet when he said, "You call this cleaning?"

Wren faced him and put her hands on her hips. She felt red-faced and sweaty and her guard went right up as she drank in the boxy shape of his shoulders. The deep brown hazel color of his eyes. The way his jaw already held a day's worth of facial hair. It matched the rich brown color of his hair, and Wren suddenly needed a very cold glass of water.

"Yes," she managed to clip between her lips. "I call this cleaning."

"There's dust on the shelves in the living room."

"Impossible," she said. "If that's true, it settled there in the past half-hour."

His eyebrows went up as if he wasn't used to being questioned. And it was clear he wasn't. "You want me to show you?"

Frustration boiled in her, and though her momma

had always taught her to clean until the customer was satisfied, she bent and extracted a duster from the box she'd brought. "I'd rather you just wiped it up." She held the blue duster toward him, satisfied when he looked at her like she'd grown a second head and told him he would too if he touched her.

Who was this man?

Your new next door neighbor, her mind whispered, and Wren regretted her decision to quip at him to do the dusting himself. She started to withdraw her hand, but he reached out and snatched the duster from her, spinning with military-precision on his toe, and marching down the hall.

CHAPTER 2

Anger bubbled just beneath Tate Benson's skin. He couldn't believe he'd come to this town out in the middle of Nowhere, Utah.

"You *wanted* to come here," he muttered to himself as he swiped the duster along the shelf, picking up a few grains of dust that mostly looked like his dog's hair. So maybe she was a good maid. He wasn't sure why he couldn't just tell her she'd done a fine job, pay her, and get his boxes inside.

Sully, his German shepherd, huffed as if he knew Tate had projected his fury about this house onto the innocent woman still scrubbing the bathroom. The beautiful, innocent woman. He cut a glance at the dog. "I wasn't that rude." But he had been, and he knew it.

He let the hand still clutching the duster fall to his side, sighing as he turned. He felt made of bone and muscle, with a simple layer of skin holding it all together. Only one hundred-sixty pounds soaking wet, he wondered how in the world he'd thought he could join the Brush Creek Police Department and fix up his deceased grandfather's house at the same time.

Tate had barely known his mother's father, but he knew this house had been sitting here since the old man's death several years back. Paid for. Free and clear.

And while Tate got a pension from his time in the Marines, he didn't turn down a free house, even if it was in the middle of Nowhere, Utah.

"Hey," he said, returning to the bathroom and startling the cute blonde for a second time. "I just wanted... I'm sorry." He sort of barked the apology at her, and she flinched with both words. "It's been a stressful couple of days."

For reasons he couldn't fathom, her face split into a grin. "It's no problem. I'm used to cantankerous men."

That intrigued him, and Tate leaned into the doorway and crossed his arms. "Oh yeah? How so?"

"I have four older brothers," she said, her sponge going around and around the sink though Tate couldn't see the rust ring any longer. "Trust me, I've had plenty of practice with being told I've done something wrong." She spoke with a note of sincerity in her voice.

"You didn't do anything wrong." He held out the duster. "It was probably Sully's hair. That dog sheds like mad."

"You have a dog here?" Alarm crossed her face. "What kind?"

"He's a German shepherd." As if on cue, Sully came down the hallway, his huge German shepherd tongue hanging out of his mouth as this house didn't have air conditioning.

Yet, Tate thought. No way he could live here this summer without air conditioning. He had a week before his job on the police force started, and he intended to put in long days to get this house livable again.

"Here he is."

Wren did a little dance away from him, back toward the sparkling toilet. "I—I'm—I don't like dogs."

Tate crouched down and scrubbed Sully's scruff. "How is that even possible?" He and the dog had been through a lot together, and Tate didn't think he could go five minutes without Sully by his side.

"He's huge," she said in response.

"He's harmless." Tate straightened, still baffled by the distinct fear he saw in her eyes. She really was afraid. He nudged the "huge" dog back with his leg and said, "I'm Tate Benson, by the way."

"I'm Wren," she said.

"Right, the woman at the service said that."

Something crossed her face, and Tate's military training told him to dwell on it. So he let several seconds of silence pass, giving her the chance to explain whatever she needed to. Instead of talking, she attacked the mirror with a glass cleaning wipe.

"I'm close to done here," she said. "It'll take a few times over the carpet in the bedrooms, and then I just need to wipe down the walls. But you can start moving things into the kitchen and living room."

Tate nodded, telling himself to take a step back. But he didn't move. She'd forgiven him for his snappy attitude, and he appreciated that. He should probably call and apologize to the woman who'd sent her too, as he hadn't been very accommodating with his timeframe for when he needed help.

"Thanks for coming today," he said. "I know it was last-minute."

Her smile was quick and revealed pretty white teeth that had obviously cost her parents a lot in orthodontia. "It's no problem."

With her pale blue eyes and that handful of freckles tossed carelessly across her cheeks and nose, Tate found his heart beating a bit irregularly. "All right then." A lesser Marine would've cleared his throat. But not Tate. He forced himself to turn and walk away, surprised at how hard it was to do.

Finally away from Wren's easy-going nature and stringent cleaning supplies, his thoughts aligned. *Moving. Unpacking.* Yes, that was what he needed to do. *Get settled. Get to work.*

The last thing he needed was another wife.

Tate stepped out of the back door and into the blistering June sunshine, a moan sliding between his lips.

Why had he decided to move into an un-air conditioned house during the summer?

His jaw tightened, and he went to get the work done. Sometimes things happened that couldn't be helped or changed, and it didn't do any good to dwell on them. At least that was what Tate's counselor had been telling him since his best friend's death only six weeks ago.

It wasn't your fault. That was what Tate had been telling himself since the accident. That, and *you can get through this.*

He paused at the tailgate of his truck and tilted his head toward the unblemished sky. *Help me get through this.*

He'd learned his faith from Jeremiah, and he wasn't going to question it now. So he looked around at the tall trees bordering the back line of his property, basking in their magnificence, and thanked the Lord for bringing him to the middle of nowhere so he could start his life over.

THE NEXT MORNING, TATE WOKE WITH THE FIRST rays of light. Something hissed, rustled, and his first instinct was to get Sully away from whatever snake had found its way into the house. He sat up in bed, the pounding of his heart almost drowning out the soft symphony of sound.

As it continued, and as Sully simply looked at him like he'd lost his mind, Tate realized the noise came from outside. He stood and padded over to the window at the back of the house. A window that needed to be replaced and then needed a set of blinds to keep private things private.

It wasn't hard to tell what the noise was now that he could see the trees along the river. They were dozens of feet tall, and the tops of them swished and swayed as the morning wind pushed them this way and that.

Tate stood there and marveled at the beautiful sound leaves and branches could make. At the serenity of this new place. At the wonder of God's creations, from the simplest patch of dirt to those towering trees along the river.

He pulled a shirt over his head and put on the pair of cowboy boots Jeremiah's mother had insisted he take after the funeral. She'd said he'd need them in Brush Creek, with Octagon, and while Tate hadn't been planning to come to this town or keep the horse at the time, he'd taken the boots.

With coffee brewing, he stretched his arms high above his head. It was nothing short of a miracle that all the pieces had fallen into place to bring him here, horse and cowboy boots and all. He had a load of lumber coming this morning so he could rebuild the porch, front steps, and the back deck, but he figured he had time for a walk.

With a thermos in his hand, he went into the backyard—which was little more than dirt and tumbleweeds at the moment—and on down to the river. The rushing sound of water combined with those rustling leaves that had woken him, and he stood and just breathed for a few minutes.

Footsteps approached, and surprise trickled through Tate when he saw a pair of joggers pass by. One lifted his hand in a wave, and Tate acknowledged him with a nod. Once they'd gone, he pushed through the chain link fence and stepped out of his yard.

"Look at that, Sully," he said to the dog. "There's a walking path here." He put himself on it and turned away from the town and toward the house that sat a bit down the road from his. It was a much smaller place than his, but it was obviously lived in and cared for. The exterior looked like it had been painted its bright white in the very recent past, and emerald green grass surrounded the house, along with well-kept flower gardens and a back deck that spanned the entire width of the house.

He passed it, vowing to be a good neighbor and get his place cleaned up as fast as possible. The next house down was twice as far away, and beyond that the river carved its way out of Brush Creek. The location of his grandfather's house had been one reason Tate had thought this town might do him some good.

The town was small, and the house sat on the edge of it. Plenty of opportunity for privacy, and reflection, and healing.

An hour later, he wore the full cowboy ensemble of dark jeans, a blue and white checkered shirt, the boots, and a cowboy hat his father had given him. Tate could still see the desperation in his dad's eyes and hear the tug of emotion in his voice when he'd presented him with the hat. "Go take care of yourself for once."

His dad had never questioned Tate's decision to join the Marines. He'd raised Tate by himself, while he served as a career Army officer. The two men knew service. They lived it, breathed it, dedicated themselves to helping and defending others.

As he got out of his truck up at the horse farm, Tate thought briefly of his mother who'd died when he was only six years old. He had few memories of the woman though his father kept pictures of her and spoke of her fondly. A sense of sadness crept through him, but he didn't have time to dwell on it because four men burst through the stable doors, their laughter filling the sky.

They seemed to spot him all at once, and their smiles stayed in place. He'd only met Landon Edmunds, and only last night. But he'd seen the row of eight cabins across the street from the other ranch buildings, and Landon had asked him about his skill with a hammer, as a ninth cabin had been started but sat unfinished.

"You must be Tate," one of the men said. He sported a trimmed black beard and his dark-as-night eyes crinkled when he smiled and extended his hand toward Tate. "I'm Ted."

"The bronc rider," Tate said, hoping he'd gotten his details right.

Ted laughed, a booming sound that made Tate want to be happy enough to produce such a sound. He swiped his black cowboy hat off his head to reveal his equally dark hair. "Oh, that was a former life." He glanced at the other men with him. "This here's Walker. He's the foreman here at the farm."

Tate shook hands with the bear of a man, remembering that Landon had mentioned something about him. The memory danced away from Tate, so he said nothing.

"And Emmett." Ted indicated a stockier cowboy with just as much dark hair. So much it curled along the bottom.

His light gray eyes danced with joy as he pumped Tate's hand. "Your horse would make an excellent barrel racing champion," he said.

"Oh, he's not my horse," Tate said quickly. Emmett's eyebrows went up, but he simply looked at the remaining man.

"Blake," he said, extending his hand. "Landon said you're handy with tools?"

"A little," Tate said. "I'm rebuilding the Hammond house on the east side of town."

"Oh, then that's more than a little handy," Blake said, exchanging a glance with Walker. "I'm trying to squeeze in construction on Cabin Row with all the farming."

"Hmm," Tate said, wondering why this was his problem. But he didn't need to be military with these cowboys. "I have a job," he said as kindly as he could, which meant his words still clipped the slightest bit. "I'm starting at the police department next week."

"Oh, that's great," Walker said. "You'll like Chief Rasband."

"Yes," Tate said, because he didn't know what else to say. Of course he'd already met his new boss, and yes, he did like Jerry Rasband, but he wasn't sure if that was because the man was bald like his father or if it was because the man had given him a job when Tate desperately needed one.

"Well, I'm just gonna...." He started to step around the cowboys, feeling very much like a fraud in his imposter clothing and boots.

"Oh, yeah, sure," Ted said. "Have a good one." The cowboys moved away, their voices filtering back to Tate. He went to the door they'd just come through, paused, and turned back to watch them for a moment.

Strong envy pulled through him at their friendship, their obvious closeness. They had things in their lives he couldn't even imagine. Families, children, wives, love, joy. Tate had experienced some of those things before, he just hadn't realized how fleeting they could be.

He hadn't realized that sometimes wives left their husbands, and sometimes families fell apart, and sometimes heartache could steal happiness like a thief in the night. He hadn't realized that all of that could happen while a man did the right thing, serving his country in a foreign land.

Tate turned away from the cowboys and pushed into the stables. Maybe Octagon could bring a small measure of peace to Tate's tattered soul before he had to return to a house everyone had forgotten about and try to reclaim it.

CHAPTER 3

Wren had been assigned to bring rolls to the midweek dinner at the Fuller household. She knew she couldn't just get grocery store rolls, so she stopped by the bakery after work for the order she'd put in the previous day.

Erin Gibbons, who'd taken over the bakery and pie shop for her aunt a few years ago, grinned at her and had the three dozen rolls on the counter before Wren could cross the bakery to the cash register. "Nice shirt." Erin tapped a couple of times on a screen and added, "Eighteen dollars and twelve cents."

Wren passed over her debit card and said, "Thanks," as she glanced down at her lime green T-shirt with a bright rainbow on it. Her mother strongly disliked her shirts, claiming them unprofessional attire for the office. But her momma rarely came into the office. Heck, hardly anyone came into the office where Wren managed the entire Fuller empire. Why did it matter if she wore bright T-shirts with cartoon characters on them? They made her happy—gave her a way to stand out in the crowd that was her own family —and she fiddled with the hem of the rainbow shirt.

"How's the new neighbor?" Erin asked. In a town the size of Brush Creek, new blood was practically a scent on the air.

"He's...quiet," Wren said. She hadn't expected Tate Benson to be noisy, and there was enough physical distance between their houses to mute him even if he was. "Don't know much about him. We haven't officially met."

Well, they had, but in a different context. She lifted her bag of rolls and thanked Erin again. The other woman followed her to the door and slid the lock into place after Wren exited. A blip of guilt tugged through her that Erin had stayed open for her. She probably got up at two o'clock in the morning to have the bakery stocked by six AM, and Wren wished she'd have come for the rolls during her lunch hour.

She couldn't change it now, and Erin hadn't said anything. Wren used her key fob to unlock her car as a truck pulled into the bakery lot. Her feet grew roots when her eyes met those dark, dangerous depths of Tate Benson's.

He rolled his window down like they were old chums and needed to chat. "Hey," he said with a smile that almost looked easy.

"I think they're closed," she said, indicating the bakery.

A frown crossed his handsome features as he looked toward the building. "Looks like it."

She smiled—why was she smiling?—and nodded before urging her feet to *move! Take me to my car!*

They listened, thankfully, and she made it behind the wheel without having to say anything else to the man. She didn't hold anything against him. She understood the stress of moving, and it was clear from his personality and the fact that he was starting on the town's police force that he was a no-nonsense type of man. Her oldest brother, Milton, was a lot like that. Milt could say something that sounded like he was angry when he really wasn't.

She pushed her glasses up and put the car in drive, pulling onto the street while Tate still sat in his unmoving truck, watching her. The tug she felt toward him was ridiculous.

"Neighborly," she said. She should've taken dinner to him on Monday. She'd known he had no food in his place, and yet she'd put a frozen pizza in the oven and relaxed on her back deck until the sun went down. The running water and breeze in the trees calmed her after a busy day at work, organizing, talking, relaying messages, balancing books, managing money—and ten other people.

She wondered what he was doing for dinner tonight,

and the thought of inviting him to the Fuller shindig crossed her mind.

"Utter chaos," she muttered. Her two oldest brothers were married, which brought their total to thirteen. And Daddy would stop by and pick up his parents, which meant two extra people and two extra dogs. Thankfully, they were small ones. Wren could handle small dogs, as they seemed more afraid of themselves than anything else.

But that hulking shepherd Tate owned? That dog held intelligence in his eyes, and he knew he could take Wren down if he wanted to. Wren knew it too and suppressed a shudder because the dog wasn't anywhere closeby.

She pulled up to her childhood home and saw she was one of the last ones to arrive. A red Buick sat on the side of the road, indicating her mother's parents would be in attendance tonight too. Which also meant Daddy had stopped by and picked up his grandfather as well as his parents.

Which meant yelling for the next two hours, as everyone in the family tried to make sure great-grandpa Alton could hear them. Exhaustion pressed behind Wren's eyes, but she stuck a smile on her face she hoped was as bright as her rainbow T-shirt and went inside the house.

A wall of noise hit her, almost causing her to stumble backward. The real miracle was that there was so much noise and not a person in sight.

"There you are." An old, rickety voice cut through the hubbub coming from the kitchen. Wren scanned the living room she'd entered to find her great-grandfather seated in a chair facing the house. She hadn't seen him because he was practically at her side.

At the sight of her favorite family member, a real smile replaced the wooden one she'd put on her face. "Hey, granddaddy." She bent down and gave him a quick hug before taking the other wingback chair beside him. "You ready for this?"

His weathered face split into a grin. "Your momma made ribs tonight. I'm ready."

Wren giggled, hoping she could love life—and eating—as much as her great-grandfather did when she was his age. The tangy scent of barbeque sauce hit her, and she heard her mom say, "Where is Wren? We're almost ready to eat and she's bringing the rolls." She wasn't sure what her mom was more upset about—that Wren hadn't arrived or that they might not have bread with their dinner.

She lifted the more important item and said, "I better take these to Momma. I'll be right back to take you for your ribs." She patted his veined hand and steeled herself to step into the fray.

Pausing on the threshold between the front of the house and the huge kitchen, dining room, and great room in the back, she took in the dozen people there. Her family. And while she sometimes felt like she didn't belong, or that she was born just to be the mediator between the four older brothers and the four younger sisters, or that she could never make her momma happy, in that moment, she was glad she had people to be with.

"Rolls," she announced, lifting the three dozen additions to dinner.

Her mother clapped her hands and rushed forward, as if the rolls were the most important thing in the world. "Hello, dear." She swept Wren's bangs off her forehead, a silent disapproval of the cut, before taking the rolls, spinning back to the kitchen, and saying, "All right, Jazzy, call everyone in."

It was casual Friday when someone pulled open the door to Jack of All Trades and paused, glancing around like there should be a big banner announcing where they were.

"Can I help you?" Wren stood from behind the desk—it did have a high counter—and immediately wanted to run for the hills. Or just into the kitchen behind her. "Tate?"

He squinted those gorgeous eyes at her and approached, each step measured and precise. "Wren?" He glanced over his shoulder like he'd definitely come into the wrong office. When he focused back on her, his eyes slipped down her body and back. "Don't you wear glasses?"

Wren scrambled for the useless eyewear and slid

them into place. Much slower, she took them off and pushed out a chuckle full of nerves. "I don't actually need glasses."

Tate's eyebrows disappeared under the brim of his cowboy hat. "Then why do you wear them?"

She wrestled with the idea of telling him the truth. "Would you believe me if I said it was to make me look smarter?" Twirling the glasses by the end of one of the earpieces, she cocked her head and looked at him, hoping he'd laugh. Or do something. *Any* reaction would be nice.

He stared straight at her and said, "No, I don't believe that."

A sigh hissed from her throat and she collapsed back into the spine-friendly chair. "Well, it's true."

"I came to apologize to the receptionist," he said, leaning into the counter and peering down at her. "Is she here?"

Wren pressed her eyes closed and took in a deep, deliberate breath through her nose. With boldness, she opened her eyes and looked right at him. "I was the receptionist that day." She half-shrugged. "Every day, actually."

Confusion ran across his face, and dang it if Wren's heart didn't start beating a little faster. Why was it doing that? Probably because of that delicious beard Tate seemed to be able to grow in a twenty-four hour period.

His current facial hair was a few days' worth and

made him look more like the cowboy he was so desperately trying to be. She hadn't seen him in anything but jeans and boots, a striped or checkered shirt, and that hat. Today was no exception, and the stripes were gray, white, and black.

"I don't get it," he finally said.

"My family owns this business," she said. "I manage it, from right here at this desk. Sometimes with the glasses and sometimes without."

He chin nodded toward her T-shirt. "But always with the funky tees."

"Oh, you like these, do you?" She looked down at the black shirt with the bright neon yellow Batman logo. It was a reverse of the usual design, and what had drawn Wren to the shirt in the first place.

"I think they'd grow on me," he said with half a smile. "So why'd you come clean my place on Monday?"

"You needed someone, and we're in the customer service industry. The customer is king." She flashed a genuine smile in his direction. "So I forwarded any calls to my cell, and I got the job done."

"Well, thank you." He spoke with a level of sincerity that wasn't hard to hear.

"Did you get all settled? The porch looks good."

A sharpness entered his eyes, and Wren realized she'd revealed another truth she hadn't meant to. "I live right next door to you," she admitted. "The little white cottage? That's me. I'm Wren Fuller, of the Brush Creek Fuller Family." He'd have no idea what the Brush Creek

Fuller Family was, but he was a smart guy, and he'd be able to hear the slight distaste in the words. Wren wasn't sure why she was feeling so overlooked in her family these days. Summer seemed to do that, as everyone's schedules turned more and more hectic, what with the town contract to maintain all the parks. That alone kept her four brothers and father busy, and Wren had to schedule the other jobs they got into tiny slots of time.

"And you haven't come over?" Tate asked after a few heartbeats of silence.

"Do you *want* me to come over?" Wren wasn't sure why the level of shock in her voice had skyrocketed.

"Maybe you'd like to see the place at a more leisurely pace than driving by."

"I *would* like to know how you got that roof looking so good."

"Oh, the roof? That was all muscle." A flirtier man would've flexed for her, but he simply continued to lean against the counter like he had nowhere else to be. He straightened abruptly and knocked on the counter. "Come by tonight if you want. I'll show you around."

Tate backed up a couple of steps, but Wren didn't want him to go. "Oh, and sorry about Monday. I'm sure I came off as a jerk."

She waved her hand, though she had found him a bit off-putting. "You were fine."

"Sully didn't seem to think so."

"Sully? The dog?"

"He keeps me in line most of the time." Tate shot

her a smile. "See you later, Wren." He turned and went through the door, taking all the oxygen with him. Or at least it seemed that way to Wren, because the air was colder now that she was all alone again.

She glanced at the clock, and the few hours until she could go home—until she could casually go next door with something sweet from the bakery, if she were being honest with herself—seemed forever away.

CHAPTER 4

After Tate left the nearly impossible to find Jack of All Trades, which was only a block from the police department, he went to see his new boss. Well, his new boss come Monday.

"Is Chief Rasband around?" he asked Lesli, the woman who ran things in the department, probably the same way Wren managed her family's business.

"Gone for the day," the brunette said without looking up or putting any inflection in her voice. "He said to give you this." She picked up a folder and extended it toward him without looking away from the paperwork on her desk.

"Oh, okay." Tate took the folder, wondering how the chief had known to leave it for him.

"He said he thought you might stop by, and that has your first assignment."

"My first assignment?" He flipped open the folder and found only a few sheets of paper inside. One looked like it had a map of Brush Creek on it. The one behind that had a list of...restaurants? Shops maybe. Local businesses.

The last paper simply said in blocky handwriting, old school-like in all caps: *GET TO KNOW THE TOWN.*

"This is my first assignment?" He turned the folder to show Lesli, who gave him the courtesy of looking at it. Quickly—barely long enough to read it—but still. She'd looked.

"Yep. Seems about right."

"How am I going to do that?"

She sighed like he'd interrupted the most important paperwork on the planet and finally gave him her full attention. "If you're going to be dealing with the people who live here, you should know how we do things."

"How you do things?" He couldn't keep the incredulity from his voice, or apparently, out of his eyebrows as they shot up. "Isn't there a law to uphold?"

"'Course," Lesli said. "But not everything is so black and white."

Oh, yes it was. That was exactly what had appealed to Tate about law enforcement. That there was exactly black and white, with very little gray. It made decision-making easier. Took the emotion out of things.

Tate looked back at the folder. "So I guess I'll go around and visit these places this weekend." He'd made most of the repairs on his house over the past five days, but he had furniture coming in tomorrow morning, and then a meeting with a gardener so he could start to get his lawn back in shape in the afternoon.

The list of businesses on the second sheet was three columns deep, and desperation tore through Tate.

"I'd find a guide," Lesli said, back to her bored voice.

"A guide?"

"Someone who's lived here their whole lives," she clarified. "It'll make the process much faster. They'll be able to tell you the hot spots, show you where the locals go, talk about who's who in town, give you the lowdown on local traditions, that kind of thing."

Tate's synapses fired at the speed of sound. "And who would you hire, Lesli?"

She looked up at him, her dark eyes glittering now. She had to be a decade older than him, but when she smiled, it took years off her face. "Someone easy to access. Someone who knows a lot of people in town. Maybe someone who's a small business owner themselves."

He blinked at her, trying to make the pieces fall into place. Easy to access. Someone closeby. Someone who'd grown up here and continued to work with a lot of townspeople. Someone who owned—all at once, the pieces aligned. "Like a neighbor."

She grinned and tapped her temple. "I knew you were a thinker, Benson. I have a sixth sense about these things." She shook her head and moved her pen down another sheet of paper, the conversation clearly over.

Tate pinched the folder in his fingers and faced the exit. So he had his first assignment. He had no idea how long he had to complete it, and he wasn't on the official payroll until Monday anyway.

He'd already invited Wren over that evening, but she hadn't accepted and Tate had seen the indecision in her eyes. He'd seen a lot of things sitting there, as she wore everything she was feeling in her expression. He actually liked it. She was a refreshing and different kind of woman than Tate was used to interacting with.

Of course, he wasn't interested in interacting with any women in Brush Creek. That wasn't why he'd come here, and some of the wounds on his heart still bled from the sudden decline of his first marriage and then the loss of the only person who had helped him through that ordeal.

Still, as he left the police station and should've turned left to head back to his truck, he turned right instead—toward the building that housed Jack of All Trades. He needed a tour guide, and Wren was the perfect candidate in his opinion. Now he just needed her to agree.

He kept a prayer streaming through his mind as he made the quick walk down the block, pausing only when he reached the door to the suite where she sat. He took the time to inhale one more time, the way he'd done countless times before his missions overseas, and then he opened the door and went inside.

This time, though, the reception area was empty.

"Wren?" he called. Music lilted from behind the reception counter, and he went that way, the folder clutched in his fist. Through the doorway, he found a kitchen—but no Wren. He wasn't sure what kind of car she drove, and with the movie theater in the building around the corner, he couldn't be sure all the cars in the lot were here for these offices anyway.

He was just about to turn around and find a comfortable spot to sit and wait for her when she came through the back door. "Oh!" The white cake box she carried stuttered in her hands, and she teetered though she wore sneakers and not heels.

Tate lunged forward, sensing whatever the box held shouldn't hit the floor, and threw his hands underneath hers. A groan escaped his mouth as they bobbled the box together, finally steadying it between them. Her side of the cardboard touched her chest, and his side touched his, and as he locked eyes with the beautiful Wren Fuller.

His thoughts tumbled, but he was very aware of the heat of his hands against hers. Very aware of the scent of her skin, which reminded him of sugar and oranges. Very aware of the slight way she gasped as she breathed in.

"You got it?" he asked, his voice rough around the edges.

She nodded, her tongue darting out to wet her pink lips. Tate stared at her mouth, wondering if she'd taste as good as she smelled. That thought seemed to bring him back to his senses, because he dropped his hands from under hers like she'd caught fire and moved back as quickly as he'd lunged forward.

He cleared his throat, no longer the strong, stoic Marine when it came to this woman. Which utterly baffled him. He'd only interacted with her a handful of times and barely knew her. But the attraction between them was powerful, magnetic, and he shook his head to try to clear it. He hadn't been this disoriented since waking up still strapped in the car he'd been driving when they'd been sideswiped.

"Uh...." He couldn't make his vocal chords form words, because nothing was receiving directions from his brain.

"I ran out to get a cake," she explained, moving to the counter and setting the box down. How she had normal functions, he wasn't sure. She opened the lid and examined the contents. "It's fine. A little smooshed on this side, but we can still eat it."

We launched him into motion. "We?" He took slow steps to her side and looked at the cake too. It wasn't safe to look at Wren, he knew that. The way his heart gonged against his breastbone testified of it.

"I was going to bring it over tonight." She shifted closer to him, and he took it as a sign that the pulse of electricity between them wasn't only on his end of things. "You did say I could come over, right?"

"Yeah." His voice scratched and came out too high. He cleared it again as a rush of foolishness herded through him. He was thirty-three-years-old, for crying out loud. And he'd been married before.

And it felt exactly like this, he thought.

Everything in him told him to get out of this kitchen. Leave the office. Get on out of town as fast as possible.

Tate absolutely did not want another relationship. He knew himself too well, for one. If he got involved with a woman, there was only one end goal: Marriage. He didn't date casually—didn't do anything casually.

Confused, and torn, and unsure of what to do, he watched as Wren swiped her finger through one of the ruined roses of frosting and lifted it to her lips.

"Mm," she said. "It's good." She almost leaned into him, and Tate really wanted her to. He could almost lift his arm over her shoulders and it would be normal.

"I have a favor to ask you." His voice was completely betraying him, as it now sounded husky and warm.

Wren settled her weight on her right leg, shifting herself further from him. "It's not cleaning your house, is it?"

He shook his head, losing himself in the pale blue color of her eyes. They reminded him of the sky over Arizona in the winter, where he'd lived while his father received some intelligence training at Fort Huachuca.

She reached out and touched his cheek, and dang it if he couldn't help himself from leaning into her touch. He realized in that breath, that single moment, that he craved the touch of another human being even though he'd told himself he didn't.

He wasn't sure what she was thinking or feeling, but her eyes blazed with intense emotion. "What's the favor?" she whispered. Her hand fell away, and Tate mourned the loss of it.

"I got my first assignment for my new job on the police force," he said, his strength returning with each word he spoke. "I need a tour guide for the town. I'm supposed to become familiar with it, get to know the customs and traditions, that kind of thing."

She inched further away and dropped her gaze back to the white-frosted cake. "Oh, well, you don't want me then."

"Sure I do."

Her eyes flew back to his, and he forced his lips to curve upward though he realized what he'd said and how it could be taken out of context. "Who knows the town better than you?"

"Probably no one," she admitted.

"Exactly," he said, almost feeling like himself again. "So you bring over that cake tonight, and I'll show you around my house, and then you can educate me on some Brush Creek history."

When she didn't say *sure, all right* immediately, Tate wondered if her past here in town was as scarred as his had been. He'd never really had anywhere to call a hometown. In fact, this was the first place he'd moved where he didn't have a plan to leave in six months or a year.

Inhaling a measure of bravery into his lungs, he brushed his fingers against hers. "I can see you need some time to think about it. I'll leave my number at the front desk, and you can let me know if you're coming."

He moved away before he acted on his insane and swiftly morphing idea to kiss her and had his number almost written on her pad of Post-It notes at her desk before she said, "Why do you need to know if I'm coming or not?"

"Well, for one, I need to know if I'm going to get cake for dinner." He flashed her a smile and finished the phone number. "And how much I need to clean up first. And if I should order pizza to go with the cake." Straightening, he looked at her fully one more time. Even in that silly Batman shirt and jeans, he could appreciate the curve of her body.

"If you decide not to come, maybe you could just text me the best church to attend on Sunday. I've seen a few around town." He indicated the Post-It notes, smiled in what he hoped was a charming way, and left the office.

He half-hoped she'd come crashing through the door and call out, "See you tonight!" with a gleeful wave. Wren seemed the type to do such a thing. But he made it all the way back to his truck and all the way home, where the windows that had been going in that morning were now finished, before his phone buzzed.

See you tonight.

His smile widened, and Tate realized it was the first genuine one he'd worn in a long, long time.

This is Wren, by the way.

"What...kind...of...pizza?" He spoke out loud as he typed, not ready to get out of the air conditioned car anyway. The HVAC company he'd hired out of Vernal couldn't come for another week, and Tate had invested in the best fans the department store here in town carried. But all they did was blow the hot air around.

Order from Pieology, her text read. *I like the Simplistic one, but anything there is good.*

Tate liked loads of toppings on his pizza, and Simplistic didn't sound like that. But it didn't matter. He could order two pizzas. *Or three*, he thought as his stomach growled.

And I want the blood orange lemonade, she added. *I can pay you back.*

He frowned at the last part of her text, surprised at how forcefully he loathed the idea of her paying for any part of this...date.

Do they deliver the lemonade? He sent the text, hoping he knew how to flirt and court a woman. It had been years since he'd been in a position to have to know such things.

They'll deliver whatever you want.

He started typing another message when one more from Wren came in.

But I'm bringing the cake.

And herself. While Tate really wanted a taste of that cake, he craved Wren's company more than any amount of sugar, and the promise of seeing her in just a few hours was a sweet balm to his weary soul.

CHAPTER 5

Wren left the office an hour earlier than she normally did, giving up at least four games of solitaire on her computer so she could stand in front of her closet and obsess.

She wore cute black shorts and a pair of strappy ebony sandals already. But she couldn't figure out which top to pair with it. If this were a date—if she and Tate were actually going to physically step inside Pieology and order there, eat there, she'd wear the multi-colored floral blouse she'd bought online a few months ago.

But she was just going to his house. Next door. Did that warrant a blouse? Was it a date if they had pizza delivered? What if she showed up looking like she'd tried too hard?

Any number of her T-shirts would be fine, and she'd be more comfortable. But maybe since she'd already confessed to Tate that she didn't need the glasses, she could show him another side of her. One who wore frilly dresses and ribbons in her hair. If her hair was cooperating, which of course, it wasn't.

Her phone rang before she could decide, and when she saw Berlin's name on the screen, she practically leapt for the device lying on her dresser. "Berlin, thank the stars," she said without bothering for hello. Her youngest sister at only nineteen, Berlin was Wren's best friend and deepest confidante. She'd be calling about something she'd seen at the market where she worked or that she'd been asked out.

Wren needed help first, so she launched right into, "So let's say you met a handsome man and he happens to be your next-door neighbor. Let's say you maybe flirted with him a little, and went and bought a cake in the hopes that he has a sweet tooth, and somehow despite all your blunders, it worked and you're going over to his place tonight. He's ordering pizza and you're going so he can show you all the work he's done on this super old, run-down house. Oh! And he's asked you to be his official tour guide for all things Brush Creek." She scanned the array of colors in her closet with a bit of dismay now.

"What would you wear?" she finished.

Berlin burst out laughing.

"What?" Wren asked. "Stop it. This is serious." She reached out and fingered the sleeve of a fuschia T-shirt that had a ice cream cone on the front with googly-eyes and a blinding white smile. Large black letters read I

SCREAM FOR ICE CREAM across the chest. Ice cream did go with cake....

"And here I was, calling you for fashion advice," Berlin said, still chuckling. "I'll go last. Tell me who this is again?"

"I have a new, *gorgeous* neighbor," Wren said. "He moved into the Hammond house. You know the one that's been abandoned for at least a decade?"

"You cleaned it earlier this week."

"That's the one." Wren turned away from her choices, her cones and rods all seeing nothing but bright pink. "I told him I only wear the glasses to make myself look smarter."

"Oh, wow." Berlin exhaled and added, "All right. So you're attracted to him, obviously, but you're not sure if this is a date."

"This is why you're my favorite," Wren said.

Berlin snorted. "I'm your favorite, because I always side with you."

Being the oldest daughter, but stuck between two groups of four siblings wasn't easy. But Berlin did always side with Wren, and she had always appreciated that.

"Well, that," she admitted. "But you're also young, and hip, and I don't want to mess this up." She hated this river of desperation coursing through her, making her stomach queasy and her fingers shake. "I haven't been out with anyone interesting in years." She could've ended the sentence with *I haven't been out with anyone* and been one hundred percent accurate.

"I heard the new guy is military," Berlin said, completely ignoring Wren's plea for help.

"He's starting at the police department on Monday," Wren said. "I don't know about military." But she did. She'd seen him pivot on his toe like a pro, and no one outside the armed forces had eyes as sharp as his. "Do you really think that's true?"

"You like military men."

"I *did* like military men," Wren corrected. Until one had broken her heart. She'd been trying—unsuccessfully—to find someone new to spend time with. But in a town the size of Brush Creek, and with the last name Fuller, the pickings weren't that broad. All of her sisters had experienced similar things as Wren. Men either thought she was unapproachable, or they disliked her on principle. What principle that was, she wasn't sure. That her family had helped establish the town? That they had money? That they lived in the ritzy section of town, with a massive park-like backyard, complete with its own walking trail, pond, and mini forest?

Growing up, she'd enjoyed the big house and the large yard. But it seemed that the men she'd grown up with that were still available still saw her as a sixteen-year-old and not a mature woman a decade older than that.

"Are you even listening to me?" Berlin asked.

"Yeah, sure." Wren blinked, trying to remember the last thing her sister had said. She couldn't. Sighing, she said, "Tell me again."

Berlin exhaled again, this time with frustration in the hiss. "I *said*, I think you should go with date attire. Something flirty and fun. *Not* a T-shirt."

Wren worried her top teeth along her bottom lip. "What if it's not a date?"

"Doesn't matter," Berlin said. "You want it to be a date, so you should treat it like one."

Wren liked the sound of that, so she reached for the floral blouse and slipped it over her head while Berlin started talking about her date.

"So let's say there's a guy you've seen come into the market a couple of times. You've never talked to him, but you've made eye contact, and maybe smiled. Then you go on break and you find out he's left a note for you with the manager, and the note is asking you out. It's only signed with his first name. You know he didn't grow up here, because hello, you're only nineteen. But you're not sure where he's from, or who he is, and you can't Google him because of the only-first-name thing."

Wren had stilled somewhere in the middle of Berlin's "hypothetical" date. "I don't know, Berlin. Sounds sketchy to me. Is he working in town somewhere?" There had been some construction on the south side of town, on the high school which was undergoing a remodel this summer.

"I literally don't know. He has dark hair and brown eyes. He's tall. And his name is Dan."

"Dan?" Wren sat on her bed. "Berlin, that could be anyone."

"Jazzy went out with that guy she met online."

"But they met somewhere, and Fabi was two tables away the whole time." Wren had been nervous about Jazzy's blind date too. "And remember how he turned out to be creepy?"

"He was a mortician," Berlin said. "Not creepy. You just find that creepy."

"Jazzy did too, and he never put that on his online profile."

"Would you?"

Wren rolled her eyes, this new argument already old. "If you decide to go out with him, get Jazzy and Fabi to go with you. Or Patrick said he was trying to get Bri out of the house this weekend. Call him and see if he'll double with you. Or go to the same restaurant or something."

"Bri's throwing up again."

Their second oldest brother had told them at the Fuller Family Dinner that his wife was expecting. Wren's mom was like a hawk and had badgered him for a full ten minutes about why Bri hadn't come to dinner before he spilled the beans.

"I'll see if Tate wants to go out. We can meet at Pieology." Since she'd come home early from work, he shouldn't have ordered the pizza yet.

"No, I think you're right. I'm going to ignore the note. If he wants to go out with me, he'll need to tell me who he is and what he's doing in town."

Relief spread through Wren like butter over toast.

"All right, then. Hey, I've gotta go figure out how to make my hair look less like a mop doll."

Berlin pealed out another round of laughter, and Wren hung up, glad one of them was amused by the state of Wren's hair.

An hour later, she couldn't stand to be within the confining walls of her cottage for another second. So while Tate probably wasn't expecting her—they'd never set a time for her to come over—quite yet, she took the cake from the fridge and headed down the sidewalk to his house.

It looked so much different though only a week had passed. He'd painted the outside a soft blue, and with the new porch, steps, railing and roof, it looked like a homey place to live. Something else was new and different about the house, but she couldn't pinpoint what.

The weeds and dead grass had all been removed from the front yard, and the on-site Dumpster he'd rented overflowed with trash and debris. Overall, he'd done more in a week than Wren thought humanly possible. The house testified of his hardworking spirit, and yes, those muscles he'd mentioned.

Her knock on the front door sounded loud in the silence of the country out here. Though they weren't that far from town, they had to cross the river and go down the road a bit, and there were only three houses out here. It was a dead-end road, and no one drove on it except her and old Mrs. Hector who lived down the lane and only went into town on Mondays to get her hair set and pick up milk.

Inside the house, footsteps approached and a moment later, Tate opened the door, his face one bright ray of grinning hope.

Wren's heart flop-flopped around inside her chest like a fish trying to get itself back into the water.

"Hey there." He put his hand on top of the door and leaned into it, scanning her from head to toe. "A blouse. Fancy."

He'd changed too, and now he wore a button-up shirt the color of pine trees. It had tiny white pinstripes and tucked into his jeans along his narrow waist.

Wren wasn't one to beat around the bush—perhaps another reason she hadn't been successful in dating anyone she'd grown up with—and stepped into his personal space, handing off the cake to him. "I didn't think a Batman T-shirt was proper date attire." She'd almost pressed past him when she caught sight of the giant dog loitering right at his heels, a tongue the size of her whole head hanging from his mouth.

"Oh, um." She stalled, her hip almost touching his. "Is he going to be joining us for pizza?"

"I can put him in the bedroom." He twisted to look at the German shepherd. "Go on, now, Sully. Back up."

The dog sat there, and Wren grinned up at Tate, a little giggle sounding in the few inches between them. She wondered what it would be like to be kissed by a strong mouth like the one he had.

"He didn't listen to you," she said.

"Back up," he said again, this time without looking away from Wren.

The dog backed up.

"Impressive," Wren said.

"We work together a lot," Tate said, finally letting his arm drop from the top of the door to slide along her waist. His eyes drifted closed as if in bliss and he drew in a deep breath, his head dipping closer to hers as he did. "You smell nice."

Wren liked the intimate touch on her back, liked the way he breathed her in, liked they spicy, woodsy smell of him too.

He came to his senses before she did, stepped back so abruptly that she almost took a nosedive into the door, and said, "The pizza should be here soon. You want the grand tour?"

Wren regained her balance, glad she'd worn the blouse and not a T-shirt. "Yes, absolutely." She looked around. "It looks so different." But he hadn't changed the carpet, the paint color, or any of the cosmetic things.

"I had new windows put in today," he said. "That makes a big different."

"New windows," she said, the realization of what was different that she couldn't determine.

"And curtains in here," he said. "And new furniture is coming tomorrow." He moved into the kitchen. "This is my mother's dining set." He ran his fingers along the tabletop reverently, but Wren didn't see any pictures of his mother.

The shelf he'd claimed she hadn't dusted held several photo frames, but they were filled with men. Tate and other men dressed in Marine uniforms. So he was military.

She swallowed and moved to the next picture. Just because he was military didn't mean she couldn't be friends with him. This photo showed Tate with an older version of himself, his father wearing an Army uniform.

He joined her and gazed at the pictures. "My mother died when I was six," he said softly. "That's why you don't see her anywhere. That's my dad." He pointed to the photo Wren had just been looking at.

"Siblings?"

"Just me," he said. "Dad never remarried. We moved all the time, all over the world."

"He was Army."

"And I'm a Marine."

Wren nodded, slipping her hand into his as they stood side-by-side in his house. Okay, so friends held hands sometimes, especially when one sensed that the other needed an anchor as he thought about his time in the Marines, as well as reflected on his family.

He squeezed her hand, and she asked, "Where's your dad now?"

"He finally retired, and he lives in Denver."

"Oh, that's not too far. You can see him for holidays and stuff."

"Yes. Yeah. You have a big family."

He wasn't really asking, and if he knew she was an expert on Brush Creek, she'd probably heard about the Fuller clan. "I'm the middle child," she said. "Literally. Four older brothers, and four younger sisters."

"Holidays at your house must be exciting."

"We get together for dinner every Wednesday," she said. "And yes, it's always...interesting." Exciting wasn't the word Wren would use, but she supposed for an only child, who'd been raised by a single father, eating with fifteen other people probably would be exciting.

He tugged her into the kitchen, and she went, listening to him talk about the new countertops, and that while he wasn't much of a cook, he'd put in new appliances too. Wren liked all the changes, and he showed her the three bedrooms, all empty save for his, where he had slathered new paint on the walls.

"So how did you come to buy this house?" she asked.

"I didn't buy the house," he said.

She turned away from the medium gray he'd painted his bedroom, noting the crisp, square corners on his made bed, and looked up at him. "You didn't buy the house?"

The doorbell rang, and his face split into a grin. "I just installed that doorbell yesterday. First time it's been used. Come on. Pizza's here." He moved with long strides toward the living room and front door, but her curiosity about the house wouldn't settle.

She hung back as he paid the Pieology driver and

accepted the boxes—way more than the two of them could possibly eat—and the gallon of blood orange lemonade. When he turned back to her with glee on his face, she couldn't help returning the smile.

Hope bobbed through her, igniting a dream she'd had since she was a little girl. One she'd thought she might have to put away for a while, maybe move to a new town to find.

And that was a dream about a life with a husband, a family, and a home with a white picket fence. As she turned and almost tripped over the German shepherd, she thought she could certainly do without the dog.

CHAPTER 6

Tate couldn't seem to settle down. His foot kept trying to tap, even though the conversation with Wren was easy, light, fun. He'd gotten the hard thing about his mom out of the way pretty darn quick, and Wren didn't seem to mind that he didn't know how to cook.

They ate at his mom's dining room table, his laughter reaching all the way up to the ceiling as she detailed all the trouble she used to get into with her older brothers.

Dinner ended quickly, and Tate was anxious to have his hand in hers again, so he stood and said, "That was some mighty fine pizza," and took their plates to the sink.

"Did you like it?"

"I love thin crust pizza."

"Me too."

"You know, I think that might be the first thing we have in common." He nodded toward the back door, wishing he could hide beneath the cowboy hat he'd gotten used to wearing. Around Brush Creek, he'd been hard-pressed to find a man not wearing one, and he'd grown quite fond of having a way to shade his eyes from the sun as he worked.

"You want to go for a walk?"

"Sure. Have you been down the riverwalk?"

"Just past your place a bit the first morning I was here." He stepped outside, glad for the tall trees bordering the river that also bathed his backyard in evening shade.

"If you go that way, toward my house, and keep going, you can circle all the way up by the strawberry fields."

"Strawberry fields, huh? I didn't know there were strawberry fields here." He waited for her at the edge of the back deck and offered her his hand.

Her gaze flicked down before she slipped her fingers into his. A sigh moved through his whole body, but he managed to keep it silent in his chest.

"I do love this town," she said, gazing up into the sky without a care in the world. "There are some things about it that are hard, but it's beautiful here, and so quiet, and a person can really just be, you know?"

"It is beautiful." They crossed the dirt that should be lawn and went down the few steps to the asphalt of the riverwalk. "Where does that go?"

"Back toward town. There're some duck ponds between the road and this path. It goes all the way into Oxbow Park."

Tate didn't want to go back toward town. "Let's go this way then." He tried not to military-measure his steps, but he did anyway. "It is very quiet and peaceful here too. I like that."

"Do you?"

"Why wouldn't I?"

"Just that...with just you and your dad, you probably had a lot of peace and quiet."

Tate nodded. "That we did. Sometimes it's not physical quiet one needs."

"Ah, so you're a scholar."

He chuckled. "I've been called a lot of things, Wren. But never that."

She giggled and adjusted her hand in his as she sobered. "So this is a date, right?"

Tate almost tripped over his own feet. His throat tightened, and he wasn't sure why he cared what label they put on the evening. Only that he did.

"Okay," she said though he hadn't answered yet. "Not a date. Got it." She tried to wiggle her fingers out of his, but he held them more firmly.

"It can be a date." His voice sounded like he'd swallowed glass and had to talk real carefully around the slices in his throat.

"Can it?" she asked.

Tate had so much to say, and none of it would come

out very easily. They passed her house, and then the one down the lane that he'd learned belonged to a nice widow named Bertha Hector. She'd brought him a loaf of bread on Wednesday, and he told Wren about that so he didn't have to tell her why this being a date freaked him the heck out.

But the words wouldn't stop echoing in his mind. They turned north, and the path went up a little hill.

"So if this is a date," he said, testing his voice and finding it strong. "It'll be my first one in twelve years."

Wren stopped walking. "Twelve years?"

Tate swallowed, faced her and caught a glimpse of the most glorious sunset he'd ever seen. "I—yeah. I went on my first date with my wife twelve years ago."

Everything itched. His arms, his neck, his throat, his feet. He hated this feeling of being covered in ants and not being able to get them off.

A nervous laugh came from his throat. "We got married a year after that, and I went to Djibouti six months after that."

"Djibouti?" She butchered the pronunciation, but Tate remembered the same feeling he heard in her voice. Disbelief. Skepticism.

"Yeah, it's on the coast of Africa," he said. "It's a city and a republic. It's by Ethiopia and Somalia." And there was so much sand there. Everything was brown and gray. Tate took another moment to enjoy the greenery around him, the rustling leaves, the golds and reds in the sky.

"I was in the Marines for a decade," he said.

Wren started walking again, and Tate went with her, hoping he hadn't told her too much about himself too soon. He'd only met her a few days ago, and since he'd been out of the dating scene for so long, he wasn't sure what was okay to say on the first date, and what he should've held until the second.

Just the fact that there might be a second date had him clearing his throat again. "What about you?" he asked. "Ever been married?"

Her laugh was instantaneous and not entirely on the happy side. "That would be a no."

"All right." He wasn't sure why that was such a funny question, but he told himself he had plenty of time to find out. After all, he wasn't stationed here for a few months. This was his life now.

"How old are you?" she asked a few minutes later.

"Thirty-three."

"So you got married when you were twenty-two?"

"Yep."

She stepped, and stepped again. "What was her name?"

"Kyla."

"Any kids?"

"No."

"What happened?"

Tate drew in a deep breath and told himself that these were normal questions. Wren should ask them, if they were going to continue holding hands, maybe share a sunset kiss....

He cleared the fantasies from his mind. "She filed for divorce when I was in Afghanistan this last time," he said, his voice almost being swallowed by the sound of the river beside them. "She said she'd met someone else and that she didn't love me anymore."

He'd expected the words to hurt—and they did. More than he'd thought they would. He'd only told two other people what Kyla had really said to him—his father and Jeremiah. Even his other Marine buddies didn't know that Kyla had gone on to get married only five days after their divorce was final.

"I'm so sorry," Wren murmured, reaching over with her free hand and wrapping her fingers around his forearm. She leaned her head against his bicep, and it felt so nice to have someone at his side.

Not just someone. *Her.*

"How long ago was it?" She slowed her steps again and paused at a bend in the path.

Tate cleared his throat. "Just last year."

Surprise flitted across her face. "So you were married for a long time."

"Nine years." Strangely enough, he'd been lonelier with Kyla than without her. He just didn't want to have to explain to everyone how he was doing all the time. And he inevitably ran into people who didn't know he and Kyla had split up, and they'd ask about her.

Being in Brush Creek was definitely better than having to deal with those kinds of conversations.

"We should head back," she said. "It's going to get dark soon, and that path goes *allll* the way around before it comes back to your place."

"All right." They started back the way they'd come, but she didn't strike up a new topic of conversation. Tate didn't either. He enjoyed the evening sounds, the whisper of insect wings, and the feel of Wren's hands on his skin.

She paused at her back gate. "So tomorrow, my brother is doing some construction on the high school. It might be a good place for you to learn more about the town. We haven't really talked about that."

"You're going home? You haven't had any cake."

"Oh, I had some." She gave him a coy smile and stretched up on her toes to brush her lips across his cheek. Fire and goose bumps erupted simultaneously, a strange sensation that left Tate immobile. "You keep the rest."

She slipped through her gate and stood on her deck before turning back to him. "If you can go tomorrow, I'm leaving here around nine."

"I'm getting furniture delivered tomorrow," he said. "Can I let you know?"

She tucked her hair behind her ear and said, "You have my number," before nearly skipping into her house.

Tate stayed on the path for another few seconds,

trying to make sense of everything that had happened since he'd shown up at her office. It seemed like a pivot point in his life, and he wanted to hold onto these memories for as long as possible.

He finally started back to his place, his fingers tracing the spot where her lips had last been and a smile curving his mouth in anticipation for when he could kiss her.

I'm coming. Tate sent the text at 8:57, hoping Wren's "about nine" meant "after nine." *Are you still home?*

Yep. Want to ride with me?

Sure. He'd managed to get the delivery driver on the phone about ten minutes ago and had learned that they wouldn't be coming until closer to noon.

He'd lain awake last night for a long time, the window open so he could hear the leaves playing with the breeze. Sully hadn't liked it; he kept lifting his big head and looking at Tate like it was unusual for him not to be able to sleep.

Fact was, it wasn't. Tate had suffered from insomnia since his first tour in Djibouti. But he was used to operating on five hours of sleep—or less—so he hurried out front door and onto the sidewalk, his sights set on the cottage next door.

Wren exited the door on the side of her house as he

came down the driveway. He couldn't help the smile that came over him. "Hey." He wasn't even sure he recognized himself. He'd thrown himself into the improvements on the house, and he'd gone up to visit Octagon every day. He'd sort of assumed that would be his life from now on. But Wren had thrown a ray of light into his day-to-day happenings he hadn't expected.

"Hey." She clicked her keys and the door on the shiny, navy blue car unlocked. He swept his gaze over it, wondering how much it had cost, and when he slid inside, it was clear the vehicle had fetched a pretty penny.

Tan leather, automatic everything, more dials and buttons than he even knew what to do with, and a large screen that came up with a menu he could barely understand. Tate had never been in such a nice vehicle, and a tremor of doubt ran through him. Her lifestyle was obviously different from his—everything about them seemed on opposite ends of the spectrum.

Once they were both settled in the car, she said, "So we're meeting my brother Brennan. He's just older than me at twenty-eight, and he's pretty fun."

"Brennan, got it."

"We'll ease you in one sibling at a time." She grinned as she backed out onto the road without even looking for traffic. He supposed there wasn't any traffic, but still. His military training wouldn't allow him to drive without both hands on the wheel at all times.

She went down by the white church a few blocks

from their houses and turned left. She drove with wilderness on the east for a bit, and then turned left and then right. Then, before his eyes, a high school came into view.

"Wow, I had no idea this was here."

"Haven't been over here, I guess." She parked and got out, waving to another man who walked toward them. He pulled off his work gloves and embraced his sister.

"Hey, Wrenny." He glanced past her to Tate. "And you must be Tate. Wren said she was bringing a friend."

Tate wasn't sure he liked the label, especially because it didn't start with "boy" and end with "friend," but he shook Brennan's hand, glad for the easy-going nature of the man. Tate didn't need an overprotective brother asking Tate about his intentions with Wren. Tate honestly didn't have any intentions. He knew he liked spending time with her. He liked how he wasn't so melancholy when she was around.

"Hey, that's the shirt I gave you for your birthday." Brennan grinned at his sister.

Tate hadn't noticed the shirt that morning, but now he found himself scanning it. The sky blue shirt had the periodic table printed on it in black, with the words I WEAR THIS SHIRT PERIODICALLY underneath. With it, she wore a pair of khaki shorts, and Tate realized he'd never seen her wear the same thing twice.

Of course, it had only been a few days, and he'd only seen her a handful of times. But he had a suspicion that

Wren's wardrobe was vast, and again he wondered if he'd be able to support her. Which was ridiculous. She'd come over to his house for dinner once, and he hadn't even kissed her yet.

But the fact that there was a *yet* on the end of that sentence made Tate's heart beat faster and his nerves a little more frenzied.

He chuckled and absently reached for Wren's hand to help anchor himself. She jolted when he touched her, like his skin was made of energy and she'd just been shocked.

Brennan saw the contact too, and his eyebrows lifted sky high. "Oh, so we're that kind of friends."

"It's not a big deal," Wren said, her voice heavy with warning. She cut a glance to Tate that said *why'd you do that?*

"Who else knows?" Brennan asked.

"Berlin."

"So it's a deal." Brennan turned back the way he'd come. "We're tearing down the old gym, and I've got all the memorabilia for you."

Tate squeezed a swallow down his too-narrow throat and then gripped Wren's fingers a bit tighter as if to say *I'm sorry*.

"It's not such a big deal that anyone else needs to know." Wren strode after Brennan, towing Tate with her.

"Relax, Wren. You can hold hands with whoever you want." He looked at Tate over his sister's head. "He seems nice enough."

"Sometimes," Tate said.

"Yeah, you should've heard him when he called on Monday and needed a maid," Wren said. "*Very* demanding."

Regret lanced through Tate again, but Wren's laughter erased it. "He's a Marine, so I guess he's used to giving orders and having them followed."

"Taking orders," Tate corrected her, though he had been a commanding officer during his time in the armed forces.

"Oh, great," Brennan said as he arrived at the construction site. "I need all those boxes moved so the construction equipment can be moved. Then I can get the landscaping started."

Tate followed his finger to a sea of boxes, some of them gaping open with picture frames protruding out of the top. "You didn't mention that I would be working," he whispered in Wren's ear. She shivered, and Tate took great satisfaction in her reaction.

"Oh, come on," she said. "You were bragging about your roofing muscles just yesterday."

"I was not bragging." He met her eye and discovered that she was flirting with him, not accusing him of anything. He softened, melted, with the teasing sparkle in her gaze.

Wren giggled. "I know. If you had been, I would've gotten to see those muscles." She reached up and touched his biceps, then his shoulders, and Tate was very aware of her older brother's watchful eye.

He stepped back, heat flaming through his whole body at her feminine touch. "How many of these can we fit in your car?" He didn't think anything besides people should be transported in a car as nice as hers, and some of those boxes looked downright filthy.

"My truck's right there." Brennan pointed to a truck infinitely closer than Wren's sedan parked on the street. "Fill 'er up, and bring 'er back when you're done."

Tate nodded, sure his face was the color of a tomato. He walked away with as much dignity as he could, but he could clearly hear Brennan say, "Wren, whatever's going on between you two is a *very* big deal."

Tate's mouth twitched, but he wasn't sure if it was into a smile or a frown. So he did what he'd always done. He dug in and got the job done. Work first. Everything else later.

CHAPTER 7

Wren could schlepp boxes as well as the next blonde woman. Certainly not as well as Tate, especially when she caught herself simply staring at him as he lifted two boxes over the tailgate of her brother's truck like they weighed nothing.

It only took fifteen minutes to move the boxes, but Wren felt like she'd been under Brennan's scrutinizing gaze for an hour. And he was the least judgmental of her brothers. And if the twins found out she was holding hands with the handsome new addition to Brush Creek, Wren would never be able to go to the family dinner again without having to answer a whole slew of questions.

"So maybe you want to take me to breakfast?" she asked, hoping he had a fast metabolism and had burned off all the pizza he'd eaten last night.

"Uh." He rubbed one palm up the back of his neck while everything in Wren rebelled against itself.

"Oh, okay." She turned and walked away, cursing herself for believing Brennan about this new thing with Tate being a very big deal. She felt something heated and charged between her and Tate whenever they touched, but maybe he didn't feel the same things for her.

"Why are you running off?" he asked. "We're taking the truck, remember?"

"Oh, right." She spun back, nearly colliding with him, unsure if she could get in a vehicle with him in her emotional state.

His hands slid up her arms, one thumb getting stuck in her shirtsleeve as the other hand traveled to her shoulder. "I don't eat breakfast." He looked down on her with sympathy in his eyes. Sympathy she didn't want.

"It's fine."

"I mean, I eat breakfast, but not breakfast foods. It's weird." He chuckled like he was the one who should be feeling anxious.

"You don't eat breakfast foods?"

He shook his head, a ghost of a smile touching his mouth. She wanted to trace her fingertips along his lips before she kissed him. Her stomach tightened with want of food—and more.

"No scrambled eggs? No pancakes?"

"No French toast, no omelets, none of it."

Wren tilted her head to the side, trying to see the puzzle of him from a different angle. "Why not?"

"I'd rather eat pizza or chips and dip."

"You're not allergic or anything?"

"No."

"So you just don't like breakfast food."

"I like cold cereal." He rubbed his hands down her arms, sending a thrill to all her extremities. "So maybe we can go through this stuff at your place, and after my furniture gets delivered, we can go to lunch."

"We can't go to my place," she blurted, thinking of the week's worth of dishes in her kitchen sink and trying to remember if she'd picked up her pajamas that morning. She didn't think so.

"Why not?"

"I...don't know?"

Tate laughed, the sound rich and round as it vibrated in her ears. "Let me guess. You're worried I'll judge you if your place isn't spotless."

"Something like that."

"Well, it makes no sense to move this stuff to my place, and then to yours." He held open the passenger door of her brother's truck so she could get in. "So how about I give you a five-minute head-start before I come inside?"

"Five minutes? Make it ten, and you've got a deal."

He chuckled, closed her door, and walked around to climb in behind the wheel. "What am I supposed to do for ten minutes?"

"You have a smart phone. I'm sure you have some sort of social media to check."

Tate gave her a long look. "Do I look the type of guy who checks Facebook?"

"You don't have Facebook?"

"Why would I? So I can tell my thirteen friends that I don't like scrambled eggs?"

Wren felt like she'd been stung by a killer bee and the poison was spreading through her chest. She had more than thirteen people in her *family*. And a heck of a lot more than thirteen friends on Facebook.

The silence in the truck seemed strained, and Wren shook the depressing thoughts from her mind. "So church tomorrow. Do you want to go with me?"

"Do you sit with Brennan?"

"Sometimes," she said evasively. "But we don't have to."

"I don't think he liked me much."

"He liked you fine." Her brother's words streamed through her head. *Whatever's going on between you two is a very big deal.*

"I just don't think he was expecting the hand-holding." She watched him, the adorable flush climbing from under his collar wonderful. "I wasn't either, to be honest."

"Sorry," he mumbled. "I—it just happened."

"I liked it," she assured him. "I just...hadn't told him that much yet."

"Who's Berlin?"

"My youngest sister. She called last night with a dating question of her own." Wren watched the trees go by out the window. "She's the reason I wore the blouse and not some silly T-shirt."

"I like your T-shirts."

Warmth filled her, and she said, "Thanks. I like your shirts too."

He looked over and met her eye, and they laughed together. Wren felt herself slipping, slipping, sliding down a treacherous path toward a real relationship with Tate Benson.

WREN WOKE THE NEXT MORNING, DRIFTING HALFWAY between reality and fantasy. She knew, because in her dream she'd just kissed Tate, could feel the ghost of his strong hand cupping her face. At the same time, she could feel the sunlight heating her neck, and the kiss had happened at night.

Her mind tumbled through what day it was, and what was on her to-do list, and if she was late for work. Her eyes popped open when she realized it was Sunday. No work. Nothing to do.

"Except church." She sat up, her emotions roaring up and curling around as if she was on a rollercoaster. She wanted to go to church with Tate. Wanted to sit by him. Wanted to secretly hold his hand on the bench between them so no one could see.

But she knew better than most that nothing was really a secret in a town the size of Brush Creek. Or with a family the size of hers.

She reached for her phone and texted him. *You sure you want to sit by me at church?*

She wasn't surprised when he responded immediately. *Why wouldn't I?*

My family will see us.

It's up to you. I don't want you to have to deal with a very big deal or anything.

So he'd heard her brother. Brennan hadn't exactly tried to keep his voice down, but Tate had walked away smoothly, never flinching, and Wren had been trying to figure out how to talk to him about their relationship.

And she didn't want to do it in a text. So she tapped the call icon and held her breath.

"Morning, Wren."

She really liked his morning voice. Slightly froggy and indicative that maybe he was still lying in bed.

"Did I wake you?"

"Nah, I've been up for hours."

"Are you home?"

"Yeah. Just lying here with Sully."

"Okay, well, I wanted to talk about—you know—talk about...us."

He said nothing, which only made Wren's nerves riot.

"Going out with you *is* a very big deal for me," she admitted. "I haven't gone out with anyone in a couple of years, and the last guy was a pilot in the Air Force who broke my heart." The tension in her chest released, and she could finally take a real breath. "So that's why Brennan said that."

"I understand."

If anyone could, it was him. So Wren nodded and faced the sun streaming in her bedroom window. "So if we sit by each other at church, you should expect to meet the whole family too. There are thirteen of us. And grandparents, and great-grandparents." She did the math quickly. "Eighteen, including me. And a baby on the way."

"So nineteen with me."

"Nineteen with you."

"I thought you said you do your dinners during the week."

"We do. I'm sure my grandma Fuller will have something for lunch. Her dad is still alive, and she feeds him a lot."

"She won't have enough for nineteen."

"Knowing her, she will." Wren smiled at the thought of her silver-haired grandmother. "And we won't have to eat with them," she said. "But you know how the pastor stands at the door and talks with people as they leave church? My family will be like that. They'll all want to meet you. Check you out. Size you up."

"So you're saying I better wear a suit."

"Do you own a suit?"

"No," he admitted. "But I could wear my uniform."

Wren's throat turned to sand. She very much wanted to see him in that uniform while never needing to have that image in her mind. She didn't like this back-and-forth war inside her heart.

"What time's church?" he asked.

"Ten-thirty."

"I'll see what I can come up with." A beat of silence went by, and then he added, "And Wren, this is a very big deal for me too, and as much as I don't want to admit it, I'm a little nervous."

"Let's just skip church then," she said. "Deal with my family another day."

His voice was very quiet and yet extremely powerful when he said, "I don't want to skip church."

"Okay."

"It'll be fine," he said. "I've met someone's family before."

"Right." The word came out without instructions from her brain, and she ended the call with an automatic "Good-bye." She made it through showering, getting dressed, and getting ready on autopilot too.

Only when Tate knocked on her front door did she snap out of it and admit that she was going to church with a man. And everyone in town would be able to see them.

She opened the door and found him on the front steps wearing a pair of pressed black slacks that were so dark they seemed to actually be sucking in the light. In contrast, his white shirt was so bright, it looked brand new. He wore a bright blue, purple, and white paisley tie, and he'd shaved his face, his sideburns, and a lot of his hair. He was very Marine. Very attractive Marine, and she wondered if she should go down this road again. After all, she knew as her heart thudded against an old scar inside it that men in the armed forces didn't stick around.

Tate's retired, she told herself. He wouldn't do what John had done—make her love him and then skip town in the dead of night instead of having a real conversation with her.

Tate reached out and put two fingers under her chin and nudged it up. "Stop staring." He grinned at her and offered her his arm, which she gladly took. "So I guess I look okay."

"Uh huh," she said stupidly, still trying to get her thoughts and emotions to gel.

"Good, because you look fantastic." He waited for her to get in his truck, and then he went around just like yesterday. Wren wanted to slide across the seat and sit thigh-to-thigh with him. So she did.

Following her instructions, he drove into town and turned down the road that led out of town, turning into the parking lot surrounding the red brick church before they got far enough to leave Brush Creek in the rear-view mirror.

He didn't seem ruffled or worried, but Wren's stomach felt like it had been taken out, turned inside out, and put back in upside down. She knew everyone walking into the church, and they all knew her.

Hailey Taylor shot her and Tate several looks before she stopped to hold the door for her, saying "Hi, Wren."

"Hi, Hailey. Have you met Tate Benson? He bought the Hammond house."

They smiled and exchanged hellos before Wren managed to slip inside. She took a seat near the back on the left, hoping maybe her family—who sat near the front and center of the chapel—wouldn't see them.

"I didn't buy that house," Tate whispered to her after sliding onto the bench beside her. "It's my grandfather's. My mother's father. He left it to me in his will."

Wren stared at the side of his face, but he seemed determined to watch the proceedings at the front. "It's been abandoned for nine years."

"I've been out of the country for a lot of that time," he said. "And my wife didn't want to move to Utah."

Pieces slid around in her head, clicking into place. "That's why you came here."

Tate looked at her, his dark eyes storming now. "I came here, because I got a job and I already had a place to live, yes. And I got that job so I could escape my life in Denver."

"Why did—?"

"Wren?" Her mother's voice could plainly be heard above the prelude hymn the choir was singing.

"Hey, Mom." She tried to communicate to her

mother not to make a big deal inside the walls of the church. "This is my b-boyfriend, Tate Benson."

He stood and turned toward her parents, shaking their hands and smiling for all he was worth. As Wren suspected, they sized him up, asked him a couple of questions, and tried to sit next to them in the back. Wren managed to get them to go up front by saying, "Berlin is waving at you." Then she collapsed back to the hard bench, utterly spent and eternally grateful for her sister.

"That wasn't so bad," Tate said.

"That was two of them," she muttered.

"And you only stuttered a little on the word boyfriend." He lifted his arm and put it over her shoulder, bringing her body close to his. She snuggled in deeper now that her parents had taken their seats. He just smelled so good, and she enjoyed the circle of warmth from his body as the pastor got up and started his sermon.

Wren didn't hear any of it, but Tate seemed to hang on every word. He stood during the closing choir number and surprised, she went with him. They made it out of the building right behind another couple leaving early, and the summer midday heat hit her when they walked out without having to talk to anyone.

"Are we escaping?" she asked.

"If that's what you want to call it." He walked fast, and she had to hurry to keep up with him.

"Are you okay?"

He slowed and looked at her, an edge of anxiety in his eyes. She'd hardly ever seen his emotions broadcast so obviously, and she traced her fingers along his jawline. His eyes drifted closed again, like he was trying to memorize her touch and needed to close his eyes to do it.

"We should go," he said, his words thick. "Maybe you'd like to go up and meet my horse?" He opened his eyes. "Or are you afraid of horses too?"

The meaningful moment between them broke, and she swatted at his chest. "I'm not afraid of horses."

"Great, let's go before I do something in the church parking lot you don't want to have to explain to your mother."

CHAPTER 8

Tate had managed to get Wren in the truck and get the truck on the right road up to Brush Creek Horse Farm. He hadn't been able to figure out what he'd meant by what he'd said.

To make matters worse, Wren had just asked, "What did that mean?"

He didn't want to be too obvious, but she had called him her boyfriend, and the reason he'd practically sprinted from the chapel was because he didn't want to waste his afternoon meeting the other sixteen members of her family. It was a selfish move, but Wren didn't seem to know. Or if she did, she didn't care.

"Pastor Peters talked about taking chances," he said, casting her a glance to see if she was willing to go with him for a few minutes. She looked perplexed. "You weren't listening, were you?"

"You smell really good," she said. "And you're warm,

and maybe I didn't sleep that great last night." She lifted her chin, practically daring him to say anything else about her inattentiveness during the sermon.

Tate chuckled. "Well, I was listening, though you smell pretty great yourself, and he said we couldn't wait around for God to direct our every step. That sometimes we have to take a chance, a leap of faith."

"All right, I'm with you."

"And I guess I want to take that chance with you. So even though I'm nervous—" Scared out of his mind was a better description, but Tate couldn't say that out loud. "I want to take a chance."

"What does that entail?" she asked.

He pulled to the side of the road, though they were only halfway up the hill where the horse farm sat. "When you touch me...I...." He licked his lips as he focused on her mouth. "I want to kiss you," he whispered, his eyes flicking back to hers. "Doable?"

"Definitely doable." She trailed her fingers along his collarbone and along the back of his head, sliding right along his hairline. Every sense heightened, and he breathed in as he lowered his head to touch his mouth to hers.

The tension between them exploded, sending sparks behind Tate's closed eyes, and he found her lips as sweet as he'd imagined. Sweeter than the scent of oranges and sugar she seemed so fond of.

She giggled and Tate let her pull back. His pulse romped through his chest, and he didn't even want to calm it. He listened to it beat out how he felt about this woman, and though it had always seemed impossible to him that he would ever want to kiss someone again, he definitely had the desire for Wren.

"Let's go see your horse, cowboy," she whispered. But she traced the tip of her forefinger over his bottom lip and kissed him again, making it so he certainly couldn't drive.

By the time they got to the horse farm, Tate didn't need the calming influence of his best friend's horse. He still had the taste of Wren in his mouth, and her hand in his, and the sound of her voice telling him that she'd found another history volume in the high school memorabilia that would help him understand more about the town.

"I stayed up pretty late last night," he admitted to her as they got out of the truck and started toward the horse barn on the south end of the farm. "I found some good stuff in a few of those books."

"That's great."

"Yeah, good to have something to do when I can't sleep."

Her fingers tightened on his. "Does that happen a lot? Not sleeping?"

"Yes," he said simply. "I have some insomnia." He kicked a glance in her direction and found the compassion mingling with concern in her eyes. "And by some, I mean every night."

"So you don't sleep?"

"I sleep," he said. "Usually about four or five hours each night is all."

"That's not enough."

"I get by." He opened the door to the horse barn and let her enter first. "Octagon is down at the end, with the other boarded horses." They walked down the aisle, but Tate didn't see a single horse in their stalls, including Octagon. "They must all be outside."

"How'd you have a horse if you were overseas?" she asked.

Tate's step faltered, and he used leaving the barn and scanning the surrounding pastures as a reason not to answer right away. "There he is. He's the paint horse with that big octagon on his side."

Wren joined him at the fence and waited while Octagon lumbered toward them. "Hey, boy." Tate held out his hand for the horse to sniff, noticing that Wren did not. She held very still and straight, and while she might not be afraid of horses, she certainly didn't like them either.

"Octagon wasn't mine either," he finally said when the horse went back to grazing. "I'm not a cowboy, though you probably already knew that."

"I suspected, though the idea of a military cowboy is kinda sexy, so...." She shrugged. "I went with it."

He smiled, his next words piling up against the back

of his tongue as he indicated the horse. "He belonged to my best friend. Jeremiah grew up on a cattle ranch in Texas, and he never stopped talking about his horses and his dogs."

"Is Sully his too?"

"No, Sully's mine. But the boots were Jeremiah's. The horse. He was full of life, always had a new joke. I don't even know where he got them, seeing as how I only saw him use computers in Africa to email his family."

Wren remained silent for a few seconds, and Tate enjoyed this more somber side of her. The side that could hear hard news and think it through before reacting.

"Was?" she asked. "Did something happen to him?"

"Yeah." Tate sighed. "He was killed in a car accident where I was driving." A missile of guilt hit him in the chest, making it difficult to breathe. Everything he'd dealt with—or thought he'd dealt with—exploded inside, and he felt like he was falling. Or spinning around in that car, the sensation terribly disorienting, and then white hot pain in his left ribs, and then darkness when his head hit the window and he lost consciousness.

He blinked, sure his skin would not be strong enough to hold this tidal waves of memories, thoughts, emotions.

And then Wren was there, putting her arms around

Tate and effectively holding him together. "I'm so sorry, Tate."

"He was the catalyst to my coming here," Tate whispered, wishing he could steal comfort from Wren. "I'd been drifting after my divorce. I retired from the Marines. My dad wanted me to get a job, but I had a little money coming in so I didn't see the point. He wanted me to come here and see the place where my mom had grown up. I—"

"Wait. Your mom grew up here?"

"Yes, of course. Right there in that house where I live now. Her name was Henrietta Hammond, but my dad tells me she went by Etta." Dark memories swam in his mind's eye, and as usual, whenever he tried to grasp onto one, it darted away from him.

"Etta Hammond." Wren whipped out her phone and her thumbs started flying across the screen.

"Who are you texting?" he asked.

"My mother." She looked at him excitedly. "Don't you get it? They had to be close to the same age."

"I'm seven years older than you."

"My mom has three older sisters. Surely one of them knew your mother."

Hope danced in his chest. While Tate had thought of trying to figure out who his mother's friends were, he hadn't quite known how to go about doing it. He had spent some time last night in the yearbooks and other histories he'd brought back to his place from Wren's, but he hadn't found his mother yet.

"I honestly didn't come here to get to know her," he said.

"But you could," Wren said. "Sort of as a bonus."

Tate slung his arm around her and said, "I thought you were the bonus."

She giggled and stepped closer to him, her fingers flying over the screen of her phone again. "She said she didn't know her, but she's asking my aunt Eliza."

"Mm." Tate took a deep drag of her hair, a new hope on the horizon that his transfer to Brush Creek would be about more than just staring over, but continuing a family line he knew very little about.

THE NEXT MORNING, HE SHOWED UP AT THE POLICE station forty minutes before his shift was supposed to start. He'd been assigned to come in thirty minutes early to get his uniform and badge, but he hadn't been able to sleep past three that morning. He hadn't been able to eat, not even the last piece of cake Wren had brought over on Friday night.

Wren was everywhere in his life, and Tate had spent a lot of time stewing about that too. Her house had been spotless when she'd finally allowed him in. The couches were leather, the appliances that new black stainless steel that Tate hadn't even seen in someone's home yet. She had hardwood in that tiny cottage, and frilly curtains, and granite countertops.

So while the house was small, it certainly had a huge budget for the interior. He'd probably spent a good hour sharing the couch with Sully while he thought if he was the right match for Wren. He'd prayed to know, but God hadn't indicated anything either way.

A vein of exhaustion from all the restless hours and consuming thoughts hit him. He shook them again, needing his utmost focus for this morning. Because just like he hadn't dated a woman in a while, he hadn't started a new job in longer. Jitters ran through his bloodstream, and no amount of deep breathing exercises helped calm him.

"Hey, you must be Officer Benson."

He'd never been called an officer, and he wasn't entirely sure if he was an officer now or not, but he just nodded and smiled. "I'm Tate, yes."

"I'm Jordan Harn." He grinned and extended his hand for Tate to shake. "I'm going to show you around, get your uniform, and deliver you to the Chief."

"Sounds great." Relief ran through him that Jordan was close to his age, with regular brown hair and eyes undimmed by too much hardship. He seemed normal, and Tate hadn't been expecting normal. Why, he wasn't sure. Maybe because every Marine he met had something horrible hidden behind their eyes. Something they'd seen in the line of duty that had changed them.

Tate reminded himself that this was Brush Creek, Utah, and the biggest scandal he'd come across in the histories he'd been reading late at night was how the neighboring town had snuck into the livestock pen at the high school and stolen the Brush Creek Bulls' mascot the night before the big rivalry game.

"Where'd you come from?" Jordan asked as he led Tate down a hall and into a supply room. "You look like a thirty-four, yeah?" He pulled a few pairs of pants down without waiting for Tate to confirm.

"My last assignment was in Japan," he said.

Jordan paused and looked at him. "You were a police officer in Japan?"

"Marine," Tate said. "I was stationed at Camp Kinser there." He'd enjoyed his time on the island of Okinawa, mostly because there were no combat experiences to be had. Plenty of amenities, including the Internet. Jeremiah had been sent to Hawaii for drills, and the bad jokes intensified via email.

A shadow crossed Jordan's face, and he stopped asking questions beyond what size Tate needed for his shirt. "You'll need black boots," he said. "There's a list of approved footwear." He handed it to Tate, his demeanor completely different now.

Tate wanted to ask what he'd said wrong, but he honestly couldn't think of anything. And while he thought it would be nice to have some friends on the force, it didn't have to be Jordan. He followed him to a locker room and got his assigned spot to change.

"Chief Rasband should be expecting you." Jordan left him in the locker room, hardly the delivery he'd promised earlier. Tate could find his own way, but he felt like just as big of an imposter in these clothes as he did in the cowboy hat and boots.

He approached Lesli's desk, noticing a vase on the corner of it. "Nice flowers," he said. "Who're they from?"

"My husband had them delivered. It's my birthday." Lesli seemed to be glowing today, and there wasn't an ounce of paperwork in sight.

"Happy birthday." He smiled at her and slicked his palms down his thighs. The pants were made from heavy fabric that didn't breathe, and Tate was already uncomfortable. "Is the Chief expecting me today?"

"Sure thing. Go on back."

Tate did as he was told and Chief Rasband looked up when he gave a cursory knock on the doorjamb. "Entry-level police officer, reporting for duty," he said.

"Come in." The Chief jumped from his chair and came around the desk to shake Tate's hand. "And you're hardly entry-level, son. Weren't you in the military for a decade?"

"Yes, sir."

The Chief perched on the edge of his desk. "You'll fit right in here."

Judging by Jordan's hot-then-cold attitude, Tate wasn't so sure of that. But he wasn't going to say anything about his fellow officer. Though his mother had died when he was young, he'd learned it was always better to say less if possible.

"So I've paired you with Dahlia Reid. She's one of

my top officers, about to move over to the detective side of things."

"There are detectives in Brush Creek?"

"We share a pair with Beaverton," he said. "And one of theirs just announced his retirement. Dahlia's been waiting for a few years for the advancement, and it should come through in the next six months." He glanced over Tate's shoulder and he did too, nodding to a slim, no-nonsense woman with dark hair and eyes. "Until then, you'll be her shadow. He's all yours, Dahlia."

She sized him up, and then said, "You're Tate Benson?"

"Yes, ma'am." He stood very still the way he'd been taught when speaking to a commanding officer.

"All right, then. We're on Oxbow today, and there's a festival tonight." She nodded to the Chief, and her ponytail swung over her shoulder when she turned to exit the room.

"She's ex-Army," Chief Rasband said with a grin. "You guys should have a lot to talk about."

Tate almost saluted before walking out, and he was eternally grateful he hadn't. After all, this wasn't the Marines—as he found out as he spent the next several hours patrolling a park while children played on slides and mothers chatted on benches.

Dahlia was nice enough, didn't ask prying questions, and taught him where teens liked to hide and tag the restrooms. But the day would've been infinitely better had Sully been at his side, and he wondered if the department had any police dogs.

When he asked Dahlia, she said, "Nope. Nobody to train them."

"Well, I could do that," he said.

She gave him the side-eye, and he asked, "What?"

"Jordan said you were brought in to take the Chief's place. Is that true?"

"What?" Tate stared at her, forgetting completely about the scan constantly rule she'd drilled into him that morning. "Where's the Chief going?"

"Rumor is he's going to retire soon. As soon as Jordan heard you were a Marine, he figured you were the replacement."

Tate couldn't help laughing. "That's ridiculous. I don't even know where teenagers like to hide in a park."

But Dahlia didn't laugh, and Jordan hadn't been super pleased either.

"I don't want the Chief's job," Tate said. "Trust me, I'm not here for that."

"Why are you here?"

"I retired from the Marines. I had a house available here, and there was a job opening. It was as if the stars had aligned." He sent a quick prayer of gratitude toward the heavens that everything had indeed fallen into place so quickly after Jeremiah's death.

"And the dog training?"

"Something I'm good at, and that this town needs."

"Oh? To aid in all of our drug busts?"

Tate simply stared at her. "If we can share a pair of detectives with Beaverton, we can share a pair of trained police dogs. They do a lot more than sniff out drugs."

Dahlia still looked dubious, but Tate didn't mind. He could bring the idea to Chief Rasband while the man was still in charge. Then, if he could train dogs to be part of a K9 unit, maybe coming to work would be a lot more than a boring walk in the park.

CHAPTER 9

A week passed. Then two. Wren got comfortable in her new routine of seeing Tate each evening. After work, she went over to his place and curled up with him while he napped on the couch. She didn't mind, but he did seem extra tired in the first few weeks after starting at the police station, and she missed talking to him.

Instead, she'd taken to murmuring things about her day and her family to his dog. The German shepherd was a very good listener, and as Tate had said, harmless. He'd lie on the floor next to the couch, and Wren found great comfort in stroking him as she told him little tidbits about her life, spilled some secrets about her family, and maybe caught a few winks of sleep herself.

Tate usually only slept for an hour or so, and then he'd wake up, apologize for napping, and they'd eat something he'd bought on his way home from work.

Then she'd go home. He seemed distant at times, but Wren determined not to ask him what was bothering him. He was perfectly pleasant—he was just tired. Still working on the house, though the projects had shifted from the interior to the exterior. Learning a new job where he claimed not many people liked him.

She wasn't sure how that was even possible, until he explained the entire force thought he'd been brought in to replace the Chief. That was about all he'd told her since starting his new job. He admitted he wasn't looking in the yearbooks anymore, and he didn't seem all that interested in finding someone who'd known his mother.

Her aunts hadn't been able to help, and she wondered if Etta was younger than her mother, or much older than Wren thought. She wanted to ask Tate, but she got a weird vibe from him whenever she even got close to the topic of his mother. So she'd let it drop.

She'd let a lot of things fall, and when she walked into her house on the day before the Fourth of July, her arms laden with grocery bags so she could make a vat of potato salad for her family's big shindig, she found she didn't have a clear space of countertop to put the groceries on.

So she set them on the floor and returned to her car for more. Her stomach clenched, and along with it, her teeth.

She'd spend the whole morning making the potato salad, and then Tate was meeting her family. The whole kit and caboodle. All seventeen of them—and that baby bump. They'd managed to avoid all the siblings and grandparents every week at church by leaving early and going up the horse farm.

He'd kissed her every time he saw her, but she noticed he didn't come to her cottage; she went to his place. He always wanted to drive his truck when they went out, though she offered to drive when he was tired. Those little details nagged at her, making her wonder if he could really ease into her life as seamlessly as she'd hoped.

Please let them like him, she prayed as she started washing and peeling potatoes. He'd already met her parents, and Brennan, and she had Berlin on her side. Everyone else had seen them sitting together at church, and someone must've warned them away, because no one had come to the back row to meet him.

Wren very nearly sliced her fingertip right off as she cut the potatoes into cubes, trying to get them as perfect as possible and all the same size. Her mother would expect such things, even in potato salad.

The potatoes were in the pot of boiling water and the eggs in the pressure cooker when her phone rang. She smiled at Tate's name on the screen and swiped a towel from the counter to wipe her hands before she answered the call.

"Hey," he said. "Your trunk is still open. You want me to close it for you?"

She darted over to the window next to the small

circular table in her kitchen and saw him standing in her carport. "Yeah, sure. Then come inside, if you want. I have leftover Chinese food from last night."

"Just that spicy chicken, or some of the beef and broccoli?"

"All of it. Those noodles you're so fond of."

"The noodles are delicious." He slammed her trunk and turned toward the window. He lifted his phone and grinned, and all the doubts and worries Wren had been entertaining the last few days dried up as he climbed the steps and then appeared in the doorway just a few feet from where she still stood with her phone at her ear.

He hadn't given her even a moment to clean up, and his gaze swept the granite countertops that were still laden with the groceries she hadn't unpacked yet. Compared to the military precision with which he kept his house clean, her place looked like a bomb had gone off.

"Wow, you need to hire a maid." He chuckled and started unpacking her groceries.

She wanted to laugh fully, but it didn't quite come out right. Truth was, she did normally hire Jazzy to come keep her cottage clean, but she hadn't dared have her come since she'd started dating Tate, because she didn't want to answer any questions.

Jumping in to help, she and Tate got the kitchen cleaned up and things put away only moments before the timer went off on the potatoes. She tested them and found them still the teensiest bit al dente, which was perfect for potato salad.

"Can you peel the eggs?" she asked, stepping over to release the pressure as that timer shrilled too.

"I think I can probably do that."

Since it was the first time Tate had been to her house since he'd helped her carry in the boxes full of memorabilia, Wren enjoyed having him in her small space. "How's the yard work coming?"

He cracked an egg and slid the shell into the sink. "Coming along."

"You should hire my dad to come put in the sod."

He scoffed. "Right. Like you need more cash to make this place more spectacular."

Wren whipped toward him, but he continued peeling eggs like he'd said nothing out of the ordinary. But her heart practically whacked itself against her breastbone. "You think my house is spectacular?" She tried to keep the extreme curiosity out of her voice, but failed.

"Sure," he said, reaching for the last egg. "It has the nicest of everything."

"My dad and brothers did all the work," she said. "We get things at practically cost." She didn't actually know if that was true or not, but she did know she saved a lot in labor.

"Exactly the reason I'm doing the landscaping myself." He finished with the eggs and added, "I'm hopeless with a knife. You'll have to cut them."

She smiled at him, though she still felt a bit wobbly inside. "It's called dicing." She set to work on them. "You can get the pickles, mustard, and mayo out of the fridge."

He squeezed behind her, both hands landing on her waist as he did, and he paused there. "Mm, there's that sugar scent I like so much." His lips touched the sensitive spot on the back of her neck where her hair didn't quite cover.

Her natural giggle came now, and she leaned into his chest. "Stop it. This has to get chilled and ready to go in the next couple of hours."

"Maybe we can skip the family barbeque," he murmured.

She turned in his arms, glad for the first time of the narrow passage between the counter and her island. "I don't think I can put them off again."

"I know." He gazed down at her, and Wren saw something in his eyes she hadn't seen before. Could it be love? So quickly?

He inched sideways and opened the fridge. "Pickles." He set them on the counter. "Mustard. Mayo. What else?"

"Salt," she said through a dry throat, turning to hide her own deepening feelings so she could finish the eggs and get the salad in the fridge to chill.

With that done, he said, "Well, I'm going to go get some work done on my yard before the picnic."

"I'll come sit on your porch." She'd been doing that

on the weekends he wasn't working, and she enjoyed watching him fill a wheelbarrow with dirt and move it, or lift a bag of decorative river rocks like they were feathers.

Today he worked in the back yard, setting pavers into a pattern to make a path from the deck he'd built to the gate in the back that connected to the riverwalk. When he finished, he ran inside to shower and she hurried next door to collect her salad.

By the time they arrived at the huge mansion where she'd grown up, Wren didn't think she'd be able to enjoy a single bite of the salad she'd worked so hard to get right.

She spun back to him at the great double doors before they could swallow her whole. "Don't try to remember all their names," she said. "And the twins will try to confuse you on purpose."

"Jazzy and Fabi. Identical twins, but Fabi still has a bit of pink left in her hair from the last time she colored it."

"Right." Wren smiled and pressed a quick kiss to his mouth. "All right. Prepare yourself."

CHAPTER 10

Tate wasn't sure why Wren was so worried about bringing him to meet her family—until she pulled into the driveway of the house where she'd grown up. As if the car wasn't enough to scream about her wealth, the house before him broadcasted it to the entire universe.

Sure, she had a big family, but this house could accommodate twenty people easily. In fact, when she opened the door, the ceilings stretched up and echoed back the conversation from further inside.

"Are we last to arrive?" he asked, his nerves making his voice lower than normal.

"Sounds like it, but I didn't see Milt's car in the circle drive."

Tate had seen almost a dozen cars in the driveway, and as he moved with Wren through the formal living room and around the corner, there were at least that many people gathered in the kitchen. Her mother directed traffic and sent this man out to put something on the picnic table on the deck and then told that woman to get the hot dog buns out of the pantry.

"Oh, Wren's here!" someone cried, and a hush fell over the crowd. Then, all at once, her siblings rushed them. She hugged them all and kept saying, "This is Tate. Tate, this is Patrick," and then "Tate, this is Kyler," Then "Jazzy," and "Fabi," moved through the line.

He shook hands with them all, hugged the girls who glommed onto him, and basically made it through the siblings in record time. He met both sets of grandparents, who wore smiles like it was the cutest thing to see Wren with a boyfriend, and then her great-grandfather who stood on shaking legs and shook his hand with firm fingers.

"Sir." He stepped over to her father, who wore an apron and wielded an extra-large pair of grilling tongs. "Good to see you again."

"Hello, Tate. How are you with hamburgers?"

"Decent enough."

"Great. Take these outside and get them on the grill."

Happy for the chance to escape, he stepped through the double-wide French doors with a plate of perfectly formed hamburgers and into a beautiful outdoor kitchen. It was covered by a deck above, so it could certainly be used in the winter, and the smell of cooking meat met his nose.

He paused and took a deep breath, feeling so far out of place here. He set down the plate and moved to the steps that led up into the yard. Stopping when his feet touched grass, all he could do was stare.

The Fuller house was indeed in an older, more established section of town, with homes that were larger and made of beautiful red or white bricks. Theirs was constructed of brown and gold stones, and sat at the end of the cul-de-sac, which meant their yard butted up against the forest and river land.

It stretched for what seemed like a mile, and he could see a duck pond in the distance. The same towering trees that he loved to listen to while trying to fall asleep stood beyond that, and they had their own walking path in the yard.

This is ridiculous, he thought. Women like Wren were completely out of his league, and he knew it. She knew it. Every man in town knew it, which was why she hadn't dated in years. Probably why her brother Brennan had shown up at church with a different woman for the past three weeks, and why all the girls still sat with their parents.

They were untouchable. So wealthy normal people didn't know how to interact with them.

The doors behind him opened, letting some of the sound out of the house and into the yard, and Tate turned to find her father, Collin, joining him in the outdoor kitchen. "Did you do this yard yourself?"

"With my sons, yes."

"And you own a landscaping business, right?"

Collin gave him a warm smile, and he certainly didn't seem arrogant or caught up in his wealth. "That's right. Wren manages it all for us, as I'm sure you know. All I do is check the calendar and show up where and when she tells me to."

Tate moved down the steps and opened the grill on the right at the same time her father opened the one on the left.

"How are you liking the department?" Collin asked.

"It's going...okay," Tate said. He hadn't found the other officers to be as warm and receptive as he'd hoped, but he got along fine with Dahlia, and as he spent his entire shift with her, he couldn't complain too much.

"Chief Rasband is an old family friend," Collin said to the sizzle of raw meat on the hot rack of the grill. "His family's lived in Brush Creek for generations."

"Yours too, correct?" Tate asked.

"My great-great-grandfather came with the original scouting party from Vernal."

"Why'd they choose to settle here?"

"The river." Collin dragged his tongs along a row of hot dogs, making them roll onto a new part to continue cooking. "And the beauty of the land. They nestled right up against the hills here, and there was shelter from the wind and the worst of the snow." He flashed Tate a smile. "Wren seems to really like you."

"I like her too, sir."

"You don't need to call me sir." Collin laughed. "I'm not one who deserves that."

Tate nodded, though he disagreed. The man had raised nine children while maintaining a family business and an immaculate yard the size of the park Tate patrolled on a regular basis.

The doors opened again, and Collin's wife said, "How close are we you guys?"

"A few minutes," Collin said over his shoulder.

"I'm sending everyone out." And sure enough, only a few seconds later, the patio began to fill with people. Wren came out near the end, her arm securely holding onto her great-grandfather's. She helped him up the steps to the grass and over to the covered pavement where the two long picnic tables waited.

Once she had her great-grandfather settled, she returned to the house, sliding her eyes along Tate's as she passed, and then came back out with her potato salad.

Tate soon learned that all the food went on one table, and that the Fullers could be quiet while a blessing on the food was made. Then the noise started again in earnest. He met Milton and his wife when they arrived, and he tried to situate himself on the end of the table, but was drawn by Wren's mother, Quincee, toward the center.

With a plate loaded with a hamburger and a hot dog and as much of Wren's potato salad as he could fit alongside them, he slung his legs over the bench and sat next to her mother.

"Tell us about your family," Quincee said.

Before Tate could say a word, Wren jumped in with, "Mom, it's sensitive."

Tate looked at her, appreciating the worry in her eyes, but he turned to Quincee and said, "My family is about the opposite of yours, ma'am. Just me and my dad."

"Oh, that's right. Your mother passed." She put her hand on his. "I'm so sorry."

"It was a long time ago," Tate said. "I barely remember her."

"How old were you?"

"Six." He stuffed his mouth full of food so he could have a moment of peace, and thankfully, Wren engaged her mother in a conversation about the shopping weekend they'd been planning. Tate only listened with one ear, and he enjoyed the food as much as he could with seventeen other people at the table with him.

Eventually, people finished eating and moved into the yard with the intention of playing badminton or volleyball. Tate hadn't even noticed the net that had been set up, probably because it was around the corner from the outdoor kitchen and not easily visible from where he'd been grilling hamburgers.

Wren took his hand and said, "Let's go for a walk,"

and Tate readily went with her, done talking for the day and they'd only been at the party for an hour.

She put quite a bit of distance between them and her family before saying, "So? What do you think?"

"They're great," he said sincerely.

"They are," she agreed, looking over her shoulder. "There's just so many of them."

Tate looked at her for a breath before breaking into laughter. He released her hand and slung his arm around her waist, tucking her right against his side. "There *are* a lot of them."

That seemed to be the Fuller motto. Lots of children. Lots of land. Lots of money. Lots of love for each other. And Tate didn't know how to deal with any of it.

BY SHEER WILL, TATE WENT TO WORK EACH DAY. HE didn't particularly enjoy being a police officer, but he got paid to work out and a few of the guys were starting to realize Tate was just like them. Wanting to fit in more than he wanted to train police dogs, he'd held onto the request he'd thought of, deciding to get a few months of employment under his belt before he started to rock the boat.

And so another week passed, and then another, and he entered the hottest part of the summer in Utah: August. He'd leveled his yard, had the concrete set to mark the flowerbeds, planted several trees, and now all he needed to do was get the sod down.

He'd ordered it weeks ago, and it was finally set to arrive today. He was awake before dawn, so he took Sully for a run down the river walk, going all the way up and around the strawberry fields, arriving back home about the same time Wren stepped out of her house onto the back deck.

"Tate?" She shielded her eyes though the sun had just come up.

He went through her gate and dropped Sully's leash. The dog had taken quite a liking to Wren, and she laughed as he hurried toward her, that huge tongue hanging out of his mouth. "Hey, there, Sulls. What are you guys doing, huh? Running already?" She looked up at him from where she'd crouched and was scrubbing Sully's neck.

Tate wiped the sweat from his forehead and smiled. "Couldn't sleep. We went all the way around the strawberry fields."

"I'll get you both a drink." She straightened, her flirtatious smile sending more heat through him. Tate, at least, drank his water quieter than Sully, who lapped and slopped water all over the deck.

"So, you're going to come watch me work this morning, right?" he asked.

"Wouldn't miss it."

So Tate took his dog home and he ate a breakfast of last night's chips and queso and didn't bother showering. He'd only get sweaty again as soon as the sod arrived, and if the loud beeping coming from the front yard meant anything, it just had.

He watched as four pallets of sod were unloaded, and he handed the delivery driver a check, which represented the last of his savings and most of what he had until payday. But this was the last thing he had to finish to make this house and land into something he felt comfortable living in and on for a good long while, and he couldn't wait to send his father some pictures.

As soon as the truck left, Wren came over and took her favored spot in the chair on the porch. He'd wanted to throw it away, but then she wouldn't have anywhere to sit when she came over.

He pulled the sod pieces off and started laying them in straight rows. The work made his breathing labored and his muscles strain, leaving little room for his brain to think about anything of importance.

"Tate?" Wren said as he started working right along the front sidewalk.

"Hmm?"

"How do you feel about having kids?"

He dropped the length of sod and whipped his attention to Wren. "What?"

"I've been thinking...and maybe you don't want children. I mean, you were married for nine years and didn't have kids."

He blinked at her, wondering when their relationship had accelerated to this type of serious conversation. Sure, they saw each other every day, went to church together, held hands, kissed...but it had only been five weeks since he'd met her.

"I'm not opposed to children," he finally managed to say. "I mean, maybe not nine of them or anything."

Wren laughed and shook her head. "Definitely not nine of them." She beamed at him like she was pleased with his answer, and Tate turned away so he wouldn't give away too much of how he felt.

He honestly hadn't allowed himself to dwell on his deepening feelings for Wren. He didn't want to acknowledge them, because he had a feeling he couldn't keep her. He wasn't even sure why he felt that way, only that he'd never felt quite as inferior anywhere as he did here in Utah, in every way. At work, around his grandfather's home, and with Wren. Always with Wren.

Whether she knew it or not, she put off a polished and put together vibe, even in the character T-shirts and flip flops. Even with the messy house.

Tate didn't want to feel superior to her, as he admittedly did while he was serving as a commanding officer. No, he just wanted to be on level ground, and he clearly wasn't. But he didn't know what to do about it.

Maybe talk to her, a voice whispered in his head. After all, she was asking him about having children, and he was sure that wouldn't be the last serious thing she wanted to talk about.

So he shifted and pushed the sod strip where it needed to go, seizing ahold of his courage before he turned back to Wren. He slowly climbed the steps, drawing her attention away from her phone.

He paused at the post and leaned against it. “Wren, what do you, I mean, where do you see us...?” He sighed. “This is serious between us, right?”

She stood, the flirty glint in her eyes going out, replaced by concern. “Yes.” She drew the word out. “I think it's serious.” She stopped a healthy distance from him, for which Tate was grateful. He needed room to think, to articulate what he wanted to say.

“You think your family approves?”

“Tate.” She chuckled, but it wasn't happy. “Of course they do. My mom and dad like you just fine.”

“That's not what I mean.”

“What do you mean then?”

“I'm a police officer.”

“So what?”

“So I just spent the last of my savings on that sod, and I don't make very much.”

Her face bunched into a frown. “I don't—they don't—”

“They do, Wren.”

“Have they said something to you?”

“No.” He sighed and sagged his weight into the post. “Have you seen your parents' house? That yard? They have a lot of money, and so do you. I'm...nothing.” He turned away from her, taking his frustration with him. “Forget about it.”

She didn't say anything, didn't call him back, but he

felt her eyes watching him as he finished the front yard and continued around the back with the sod. And no matter how hard Tate worked, he couldn't outrun the thoughts that not only was he nothing, he had also nothing to offer her. And the reason she hadn't called him back to keep talking was because she knew it too.

CHAPTER 11

Wren stayed on Tate's front porch as he moved around the back, a second away from crying. Just when she thought she had her emotions under enough control to go talk to him, she'd be unable to breathe without a hitch.

He worked like a dog, never stopping, never taking a break, though it had to be hovering close to one hundred degrees today. She was hot sitting in the shade and Sully panted at her side like he'd just run another five miles.

Finally Tate came around the front and said, "Help me with the sprinklers, would you?"

She nodded and got up, her legs feeling stiff and gelatinous at the same time. Was he going to break up with her? Who would she sit by at church tomorrow?

She shook the stupid thought out of her head. Tate

had become a lot more than a pew partner, and she knew it. Her heart ricocheted around inside her chest at what might happen next. She found him around the back corner of the house, peering into a small green box attached to the siding there.

"So this is the front." He pointed to a button labeled with a simple number one. "And the side, all the way to the fence." The number two. "And the back yard." Number three. "I'm going to go to that corner and have you push the buttons to see what happens. Okay?"

The nearness of him made Wren soft in the bone marrow, but she managed to nod. He walked away, single in his purpose to get his yard up and running. She wished she had his drive, his hardworking spirit, and she wished she knew exactly what he was thinking so she could right it.

"All right," he called, barely glancing at her. "Just the front yard."

She pushed the button, expecting a beep, a hiss, something. Nothing happened. "Did it go?" she asked.

"Did you push it?" he called.

"Yes!"

He twisted toward her and back to the yard. "Oh, here it is." A few moments later his laughter filled the summer sky, painting Wren's life with gold warmth she wanted to hold onto forever.

"All right. Turn that one off." He turned but stayed at the front corner. "Turn on the side here."

She pushed the two and this time, she did hear a sputtering hiss before the sprinkler heads popped up out of the ground and started clickety-clacking around to water the lawn.

"And off." Tate started walking toward her almost before she could switch off the sprinklers, and he pushed the number three when he arrived back at the meter.

He looked at her, pure joy radiating from his face. "They work."

"Of course they do." She tried a smile on her face, but it wobbled. She wrapped her arms around him as he chuckled, relishing the vibrations as they passed from his body and into hers. He stroked her hair, and whenever he did, it was the only time she liked her hair.

"Are we okay?" she asked him, still holding very tightly to him so she wouldn't have to look him in the face.

"Yeah," he said, but it wasn't delivered with any sense of weight behind the word.

"What are you thinking?" she asked.

"I already told you what I'm thinking." He stepped out of her embrace and ducked his chin toward the ground. "I need to get the sprinklers on for a while and take a shower. Then we can go grab something to eat."

He pushed all the buttons, letting his gaze slide right past her, and then turned to go inside. "You can wait with Sully, if you want."

She had before. Several times. But for some reason, now she felt a skin of strangeness tightening over her as she thought about stretching out on his couch, her phone in her face, while he showered.

"I'll go...do something." She headed down the paved path he'd done a couple of weeks ago and onto the riverwalk. When she looked back, she half expected to see him standing there, his hands tucked in his pockets, watching her.

He was gone.

WREN BEGGED OUT OF LUNCH THAT DAY, CLAIMING the sun had given her a headache. She went to church with Tate, and that distance she'd noticed over the Fourth of July returned. Though neither of them acknowledged it or said anything, Wren had a hollow pit in her stomach for most of the day. By the time she showed up to work on Monday morning, she wasn't sure she could go through another day without clearing the air between her and Tate.

But her day started out busy, with a customer calling in a new job that Wren had to pull Patrick over to, and another one calling with a complaint about one of Fabi's jobs from over the weekend.

By lunchtime, Wren wanted to take the next month of Mondays off, so when someone pushed into the office, she had her angry gaze on—until she saw Tate in all his uniformed glory. She'd never seen him in his black police uniform, but she'd heard him complain about the fabric. She really liked it, and her heart kicked into a new gear when their eyes met.

Her anger melted into fear. She stood as he approached with a white bag from one of their favorite go-to places for the best fast casual Italian food in town, Italy Red.

"I brought you the fifty-fifty." He set the bag on the counter and smiled at her. Maybe everything was fine. He wasn't acting strange today, though the past two days had been filled with tension and the fear of the unknown.

"Thank you." She smiled at him. "It's good to see you. It's been a crazy morning."

"Well, hopefully this will make your day better."

"You didn't get anything for yourself."

"They're feeding us at the station today. I guess it's Cory's birthday."

"Oh, right. Cory Patton. He's Brennan's age."

A strange look crossed Tate's face, but Wren saw it. She'd gotten good over the past several weeks at reading the minute clues he allowed through the mask he usually wore. And this one said he didn't like that she knew Cory Patton and how old he was.

But she couldn't change that. Just like she couldn't change who her family was, or where they lived, or how much money they had.

"Look, Wren." His voice sounded like he'd gargled with glass.

"Don't," she said.

"I just don't see how this is going to work out." He looked at her fully now, all of his emotions streaming through the mask. "I laid awake for hours last night, trying to figure things out. And I can't get past the fact that guys like me don't end up with girls like you."

The once tantalizing scent of the marinara with the Alfredo sauce made her nauseous. "Yes, they do."

"No, Wren, we don't."

"I'm just a normal woman."

He shook his head, a sadness entering his face she really disliked. "Wren, you're anything but normal." His hand flinched toward her, as if he'd cup her face and draw her in for a kiss like he'd done so many times before.

Instead, he fell back a step. "I can't give you the kind of life you're used to, and it's not fair to either of us to expect me to."

"I never said anything about the kind of life I'm used to." She wasn't even sure what that meant. Did she hurt for money? No. If something broke, her dad could fix it, or her dad knew someone who could. If she wanted a new couch or a new bed, again, her father knew someone who could help her, get her a deal, something.

"But you did, Wren." He moved back another few

steps. "You did." And just like that, in only the moment it took her to inhale, he was gone.

Wren fell back into her ergonomic desk chair, unable to stay standing without him in her life.

"Did that really just happen?" She stared at the door as a chill descended on her skin, usually welcome this late in the summer but which now left her feeling clammy and cold inside as well as out.

CHAPTER 12

Tate shuffled through the rest of his day, and then the week. When the weekend came, he had nothing to do around the house as he'd finished the yard last weekend and all the major projects had been completed for a while now.

He wished he could simply sleep until the pain of missing Wren went away, but he wasn't sure it ever would. He'd been growing apart from Kyla for three years before he opened an email and found their house had been listed for sale and divorce papers in the attachment.

Jeremiah had been right beside him, messaging his mother about something that had made him laugh. Tate could still distinctly hear that laugh, and another intense wave of missing rolled over him, this time for his best friend.

He'd hoped to be able to make some friends here in Brush Creek, and a few of the other officers were finally coming around, especially Cory.

Someone knocked on the door, almost making Tate spill to the floor in surprise. How long he'd been lying on the couch, he wasn't sure. And who could possibly be on the other side of the door, he didn't know.

But Sully seemed eager for him to get the door, so he heaved himself to his feet and moved them to the door. He almost called out, "Who is it?" but he never had before, not even when he lived in a much bigger city. So he simply opened the door and braced himself.

"Tate." His father's tall frame filled the doorway, and everything in Tate sighed in relief.

"Dad." He stepped into his dad's arms and took the hearty pounding on the back with joy. "I forgot you were coming this weekend."

"You forgot?" His dad pulled back and looked at Tate. "I don't think you've ever forgotten anything." His eyes saw everything, including the fact that Tate still wore his pajamas and hadn't shaved since Monday.

"Yeah, well, I'm not the same person I used to be." He turned, the instantaneous joy he'd felt only a moment ago gone.

His father followed him inside and closed the door against the heat. "Are you all right?"

Tate collapsed onto the couch and ran his hands along his face. "I've been better."

"Are you sick?"

If having a broken heart counted, then yes, Tate was very, very sick. He looked up, realizing the concern in his father's face. "I'm okay, Dad. Just...getting over something." He'd never mentioned Wren to his father, though the excitement of falling in love and wanting to shout it from the rooftops had existed.

"Well, the house looks great," his father said, glancing around and stepping into the kitchen. "It was never this nice when your grandfather lived here."

"Did you come visit?" he asked.

"A few times, sure." His dad went down the hall. "This was your mother's room." He paused in the first room on the right side of the hall, directly across from the bathroom. "And I see you took the master."

"It connects to the bathroom," Tate said. He had no idea what time it was, but his stomach seemed angry he hadn't fed it yet. "Dad, let's go get something to eat."

He came back down the hall, his broad shoulders practically touching both walls in the old farmhouse. "The yard looks great. The sod took real nice."

"That it did. You were right. Lots of water and it dug right in." He'd consulted with his father about everything in the house, from how to replace a toilet to how to build a deck.

"Is that Italian place still in business?"

"Italy Red?" His throat nearly closed off thinking about the last time he'd been there. "Yeah." He cleared the emotion from his voice. "Yep, it's still open."

"They have the best spinach and mushroom calzone in the world." His dad grinned, full of life and happiness, despite some of the hard things the universe had thrown at him.

Tate wished he could be more like him, but he felt like he'd been dealt so many unfair things in the past several months that they were still all yoked around his shoulders. And they were so heavy.

"Let me shower, and we'll go." Tate edged past his dad, taking care not to look directly into his eyes so his father couldn't see the depth of his misery. With any luck, the spaghetti and meatballs could give him just a few minutes of reprieve.

By the time they sat across from each other in the booth at Italy Red, Tate knew he only had minutes before his father would dig down to what was really going on.

Sure enough, his dad chattered about the happenings in Shiloh Ridge, the small mountain town at the base of some mountains in Colorado. His father managed the sporting goods store there, such a far cry from what he'd done his whole life that it almost seemed...normal.

For the first time since he retired from the Marines, Tate thought he might be able to be normal someday too.

"So what's eatin' at you?" his dad finally asked, half of his food gone. "I've been talking and talking and you've barely said two words."

Tate looked at the only member in his family. The man who'd loved him unconditionally and raised him the best he could. "I'm dealing with a lot of...loss," he finally said, not quite sure of the last word until he said it.

His dad nodded. "Retiring can be really hard."

Tate did miss the Marines, though he'd never acknowledged those feelings. He'd kept in touch with a few of his buddies, but when Jeremiah had died, Tate had cut off all contact with anyone who reminded him of the Marines, who reminded him of what had happened, who reminded him that he'd killed his friend.

"Have you seen someone here about Jeremiah?" his dad asked.

Tate pressed his lips together and shook his head.

"Tate, you said you would." His dad spoke with kindness, but an undertone of frustration. "You don't have to deal with things on your own."

"I know, Dad. It's just been a rough transition." He hadn't sought out a new counselor here, because he'd met Wren. She'd soothed his soul, given him something to smile about each day, and provided the mental and emotional therapy he needed. Without her, though, Tate felt the same darkness he'd brought to Brush Creek with him infecting his whole soul again. No amount of prayer had helped, and Tate felt utterly abandoned. Again.

"You work too hard on things," his dad said. "You get obsessed with them until they're finished. No one should've been able to take that house in that condition and do what you've done in only six weeks."

Tate conceded the point, though he didn't think he'd worked obsessively on the house. He'd worked on it every chance he got. Was it wrong to want somewhere clean and comfortable to live?

"How are things going at the station? Getting better?" His father reached for his water—never soda for him—and drank almost half the glass. He never drank during the meal, only after, and Tate's heart warmed for the consistency of his dad. How predictable he was. How genuine.

"A little better each day," Tate admitted. "I think everyone finally realizes I didn't come here to take over for the Chief, and they're opening up to me a little." Again, he hadn't worried too much about his lack of friendships at work, because he'd had Wren. Everything about his new life in Brush Creek seemed to revolve around her, as if she was the bright, shining star of this place. Without her, he felt lost, alone, and distant from everyone.

"So what is it, really?" His dad leaned forward, those Army intelligence eyes looking for what normal people couldn't see.

Tate's heart beat way too fast. If he started talking about Wren, he had no idea how much he'd say. "I don't know," he said, knowing his father wouldn't stand for that.

You know. Just think about it and say it. Tate thought

the phrases from his childhood as his dad said them out loud.

He didn't need to hide anything from his father. Tate wasn't worried about that. No, he was concerned that he'd been lying to himself all this time, and he'd have to confront feelings he didn't know how to deal with.

"I met a woman," he said, looking evenly into his father's eyes. "And we broke up earlier this week."

His dad blinked, clearly not expecting Tate to say anything about a girlfriend. "What was her name?" he asked.

"Wren Fuller." Tate almost whispered the words, sure every other patron in Italy Red would seize onto the information about their breakup and spread it around town. As if they didn't already know. He was well-versed in small town mechanics now, and he'd learned through his service on the force that someone around town had always seen something. Someone always knew someone else, even if they were just passing through town.

Dahlia had taught him there were eyes and connections everywhere, and he had to know where to look and who to talk to in order to get the information he needed.

"Wren Fuller." His father said the name as if he was searching his memories for Wren. "She must be Quincee and Collin's daughter."

"That's right," Tate said, not even a little surprised

his father had been able to come up with their names. He was exceptionally gifted at remembering names, dates, and tiny details about things. He'd trained to do it and then had executed that training for thirty years in the Army.

"Where did you meet her?"

"She owns the cottage next door." He pushed his meatballs around his plate, wishing he cared enough to eat them.

"You like her?"

Tate couldn't help nodding, the misery he'd kept at bay all week flooding him now. "Very much."

"You fell in love with her?"

Tate's gaze flew from the plate of spaghetti to his father's eyes, panic rearing inside him now. He hadn't allowed himself to answer that question, though he knew exactly what love felt like. He'd experienced platonic love for his dad. Romantic love with Kyla. Brotherly love for Jeremiah.

How did he really feel about Wren?

"I can see you don't really know," his dad said. "You should probably figure it out. If you love her, whatever happened between you can probably be fixed."

Tate thought of her enormous, loud family, wondering if he'd ever be able to find a place to fit among them. An image of the Fuller's house, their material possessions, and that huge backyard taunted him. He would never be able to provide Wren with much more than he currently had.

She wanted children—he did too. Could he even afford to pay to raise a family on the meager income he got from his police work? He wasn't sure, but the few paychecks he'd gotten sure had seemed to go quickly, and it was just him right now.

"What if I love her?" Tate asked. "So what? I was in love with Kyla too, and that didn't last."

Sympathy filled his father's eyes and he extended his hand across the table to pat Tate's. "Son, there are different levels of love. I have no doubt you loved Kyla, and she loved you too, at least for a little while."

"Are you saying she didn't love me enough?"

His dad cocked his head to the side. "Yeah. She didn't love you enough to stick around with things got hard. Maybe Wren does."

Tate found it laughable that Wren would love him at all. What did he bring with him? Emotional baggage from a broken first marriage. Anger and agony over the loss of a best friend. A barking voice when he got too tired or things didn't go his way. And a dog she didn't like.

She likes Sully, he told himself.

"Is that why you never got remarried?" Tate asked. "You didn't love someone enough?"

A bright sadness entered his father's expression. "I loved your mother in a way I could never love someone else," he said. "She's part of the reason I never searched out another companion. The other was you. I had you, and I enjoyed taking care of you, and I didn't want to complicate things for you." He drained the rest of his water. "So all of that, plus we moved constantly. It was hard to meet single women and maintain a relationship for much longer than a few months." His dad shrugged one powerful shoulder. "I was fine with it."

"Was?"

A hint of redness crept into his dad's face. "I'm seeing someone in Shiloh Ridge."

Tate's surprise shot through the roof. "What's her name? Tell me about her."

And as his father talked about Judy Simmons, Tate finally found a way to relax. To smile. To be more like the man he'd been since coming to Brush Creek and meeting Wren.

He wasn't sure what that said about her, or about his father, but he was able to enjoy the rest of the weekend with his dad, the thought of Wren always hovering at the back of his mind. There, but not consuming him. It was a beautiful reprieve that fled the moment his father climbed behind the wheel of his truck and put Brush Creek in his rear-view mirror.

Tate stood on his front porch, the Monday morning sun already awake and heating things up. He allowed himself one quick glance at the white cottage next door. He did, because he knew he wouldn't see Wren this early in the morning.

But her house embodied her, and the taste of bitter sadness made him turn away and go quickly inside, where the only reminder of Wren was the puppy dog eyes Sully wore.

"I know," Tate told the dog. "I'm thinking of something." He just needed more time to figure out how he felt, and then what to do about it.

CHAPTER 13

Wren didn't even check to see what was on her T-shirts anymore. She put on jean shorts, or black shorts, or khaki shorts, and reached blindly into her closet for a shirt to go with. No one came into the office, and no one came over to her house, and no one would even know if she got in her car and drove for hours.

She thought about doing just that, wondering how long it would take before someone noticed she wasn't in town anymore.

It would probably be her mother who would discover Wren's absence first. Once she'd learned that Wren and Tate had split up, she'd called every day. Sometimes twice a day, as if Wren needed a wake up call to get up and go to work.

As zombie-like as she'd become in her routines of showering, getting dressed, eating breakfast, and driving to the office, maybe she did need that seven o'clock call to get her out of bed. She certainly didn't feel like doing anything voluntarily. Not anymore.

The idiotic tears that had been instant whenever she thought about Tate, or what she couldn't do with Tate that night, or why she couldn't pop over to see him, sprang to her eyes once more. And why? Because she heard Sully bark three times.

That silly dog had wormed his way into her heart too. She took a quick peek out the window and saw Tate's truck rumbling down Traverse Road away from their houses. So that was why Sully had barked.

Wren felt the same way. She wanted to bark and bellow and beg him to come talk to her. For them to work things out.

Instead, her phone rang and her mother's picture appeared on the screen. Wren didn't dare send it to voicemail. Her mom had told her if she didn't answer, she'd send someone over to the cottage to make sure Wren was okay.

"Hey, Mom." Wren turned away from the window.

"Sweetheart. You sound good today."

A façade. A front. Anything to convince herself her job mattered, that someone would miss her if she got in the car and drove.

"I'm doing okay," Wren said, pulling out a container of cream that wasn't for her coffee.

"Fabi and Jazzy are bringing dinner to you tonight."

"Mom, that's not necessary." She'd been eating fine

since Tate's departure from her life. For the past ten days, she'd eaten everything in sight. Even now, she pulled out a box of cereal and poured herself at least two servings, covering them in pure, white cream before taking the bowl to the living room couch to eat.

"Well, it's their birthday in a few days, and they want Pieology. Since you're the only one who really likes that place, they thought they'd bring some over and celebrate early with you." Her mother cleared her throat. "Because we're all assuming you won't come to the birthday dinner next week?" She phrased it like a question, but it wasn't really one.

"No," Wren said, the very idea of getting together with her obnoxious family without Tate to anchor her absolutely horrifying. "I'm sorry, Mom. I just don't think I can right now."

"I know, dear," her mother said in a rare showing of understanding. She'd been great after John had deserted them all too. At least Wren wasn't to the diamond-wearing stage with Tate, as she had been with John.

"Pat says he'll get arrested, just so you have a reason to stop by the station and see Tate."

A strangled laugh came out of Wren's throat. "That's not necessary." She could see him anytime she wanted. All she had to do was go next door and demand he explain things better. She could explain more about her expectations for her life—if she knew what they were. She'd grown up in the family business. She knew how to run it. She had the degree her parents had paid for. And honestly, she enjoyed what she did about ninety percent of the time.

But did she have unrealistic expectations for a husband? That he would be able to provide the same kind of life for her that her father had—and still did?

Wren wasn't sure. So she said her goodbyes to her mother and headed out the door to the office. Until she knew what she truly expected of Tate, she wasn't going to go get her heart stomped on again. After all, he wore very large black boots, and her most vital organ was still weeping a little bit from the lashing it had taken ten days ago.

She left the office earlier than normal so she could get home before Tate. The police department operated like clockwork, and he finished at five-thirty come rain or shine. She didn't like driving past his house and seeing his truck parked in the driveway, knowing she couldn't just hop on over there and kiss him.

She'd just stepped into a pair of fluffy pajama pants when she heard knocking on the door and her sister's voice calling, "We're coming in!"

Wren squeezed the last bit of water from her hair and went to greet Fabi and Jazzy. "Hey, guys." She hugged Fabi first, the more emotional of the sisters, and she hung on tight. "Happy birthday."

"Forget about that." Fabi moved back and held

Wren at arm's length. "We already know you didn't get us anything. How are you?"

"I did too get you something." She took the few steps to the dining room table, which held a lot more than the two gift bags she'd put together on Sunday while she was avoiding the church. She didn't think Tate would skip, no matter the price of seeing her, so she'd given them both the relief and stayed away.

It had been the perfect time to drive to Vernal anyway. Hardly anyone on the road, and practically the whole department store to herself.

"This one's for you." She handed the purple bag—Jazzy's favorite color—to one sister. "And this one's for you." She presented a much smaller bag in blue and green to Fabi.

Jazzy and Fabi exchanged a look, and Fabi, the older of the twins, opened her bag first. A black box sat inside, and she pulled it out. "I know what this is."

"No, you don't." Excitement built in Wren. Sure, Fabi liked the charm bracelets that were popular these days. She owned so many she couldn't even wear them all at once.

She cracked the lid on the box and gasped. "Wren." Her wide eyes met her sister's, then her twin's. "It's the memory chain I've wanted."

"Go on," Wren said, smiling fully for the first time in days. "Let me help you put it on."

Fabi reverently took the necklace out of the box and allowed Wren to sweep it around her neck. "I got you three memories," she said softly as Fabi held up her hair. "The butterfly is to remember to fly. The hot air balloon is to remind you to lift others. And the heart is to remember how much your family loves you."

When Fabi turned, she had tears in her eyes, and since Wren's emotions lingered on the surface of her skin, she cried too. "Thank you, Wren."

She stepped back, sniffing. "All right, Jazzy. Your turn." Wren wiped her eyes, wishing Jazzy had gone first. She was infinitely harder to shop for, and Wren usually gave her a gift card to her favorite online boutique. But as she'd wandered the aisles at the department store for hours, she'd had the time to really search for something.

Jazzy removed the tissue paper from the bag and then pulled out a box, her face brightening into a smile. "Yes!" She grinned and giggled. "Wait. Is this really what it is?"

Wren nodded, glad her gifts had brought her sisters some measure of happiness. Like lightning, she realized that her own mood had lifted by serving others. Her own attitude had changed, just for a few precious minutes. And while she managed a business that relied on helping others, she'd never viewed what she did as service or helpful.

She also knew she needed to be more giving and think less of herself and her own wants.

"So tell us about Tate," Jazzy said as she fiddled with the bright pink alarm clock that she could dock her iPod with. She'd wanted one for a while now, because she wanted to wake up to her favorite songs, not "some DJ talking about the weather."

"I don't know about Tate," Wren said, suddenly ravenous for a whole thin crust pizza. She put three slices of the Simplistic pizza on her plate. Just cheese, pepperoni, sauce, and bread, the pizza was divine.

"What don't you know?" Fabi asked, loading her plate with food too. "You really seemed to like him."

"Why'd you guys break up?" Jazzy abandoned her present and joined the other two sisters in the kitchen.

"Why do all men break up with us?" Wren asked.

"We were on our best behavior at the picnic," Fabi said. "And you guys dated for a few weeks after that."

"So then...."

"Money?" Jazzy asked. "Doesn't he have a lot of money? I mean, look at what he's turned that house into in like, what? A week?"

Wren smiled, because though it had definitely been a lot longer than a week, Tate had transformed the broken down farmhouse next door into something magnificent rather quickly.

"I don't know how much money he has," Wren said. "I don't really care." As she spoke the words, she realized how true they were. "I've never screened my dates based on their income."

"Oh, I do," Fabi said, fingering the balloon charm around her neck. And she was serious too. Fabi wanted someone who would spoil her rotten, and she rarely went on second dates because of it.

"I know you do, Fabs." Wren finished a slice of pizza and found she couldn't eat any more. "I think I just need something to do. Somewhere to spend my time that isn't about me."

"Like the Salvation Army or something?" Jazzy looked at Wren like she'd lost her mind. "That's all the way in Vernal."

"And they pay their people," Wren said. "No, I'm talking about volunteering somewhere. Just...doing something for someone else."

"Well, Pastor Peters always says he's looking for people to visit the elderly."

Wren cracked the top on a soda, her mind churning. There had to be opportunities to serve right here in Brush Creek. She just needed to find them, whether that was civilly or religiously.

"I'll call him," she told her sisters, and the conversation turned to something lighter. Wren's thoughts never strayed far from Tate and how she could be the kind of woman who didn't come across as one who demanded the best of everything.

She honestly wasn't that person, but she'd obviously made him think she was. *If I can fix that*, she thought. *I can get him back.*

Please help me get him back.

CHAPTER 14

Tate stood from the kitchen table, taking a moment to admire the scratches in the top of it. He hadn't spent much time seeking out his mother, but in that moment, with one fingertip tracing down one particularly large gouge, time held still. He felt her close to him, a sensation he'd had several times throughout the three decades she'd been gone.

"I don't know, Mom," he whispered, his eyes moving back to the notebook he'd been scrawling in. "Even with this budget, it would be hard to have babies."

Wren could work.

Tate sighed. "Yeah, I know." She could probably take the babies to the office with her. From what he'd seen, she sat behind a desk and played computer card games. Sure, she worked too, managing schedules, updating calendars, taking care of payroll, and income, and a thousand other things, he was sure.

Do you love her?

It wasn't his mother asking, but a question that had been on his mind for days. What would happen if he admitted that yes, he loved her?

"I don't know," he said. "But I know I'm horribly miserable without her."

Then go fix it.

The numbers he'd printed in his cramped handwriting mocked him, and he ripped the page from the notebook and headed for the front door. Sully looked up, his eyes bright and curious.

"Yeah, come on. Let's go talk to Wren."

But instead of walking next door and facing the woman he thought he might be in love with, he jumped in his truck and headed into town. He couldn't show up empty-handed, not with a woman like Wren.

He also couldn't leave Sully in the truck in this heat, so he grabbed the dog's leash and towed him into the department store with him. The funny part was, no one said a single word to him. After finding the women's section, he realized quickly Wren didn't buy her funky T-shirts here.

He flagged down someone wearing a nametag that read Jordanna. "Hey, so I'm looking for a bright T-shirt. You know, with characters and rainbows and stuff on them."

"Just around the wall there. There's a whole spread of them." She grinned at him, and he thanked her before taking Sully around the wallet displays. Sure enough, an entire wall held cubbies of the exact kind of T-shirts Wren wore.

Good thing they had them all displayed above the cubbies, with numbers pinned to the corner so Tate could easily find what he was looking for. But he felt like he was navigating a minefield—which he'd actually done before.

Too many choices.

"Okay, Sully," he said. "What do you think Wren would like?" He moved away from the purple. "Not purple. She said it doesn't look good with her hair." Tate wasn't exactly sure what that meant, but he didn't want to show up on her doorstep after three weeks with the wrong color of shirt, he knew that.

He'd seen her wear black, yellow, pink, and blue. As he spied an orange shirt, more the color of a creamsicle than a cantaloupe, his heart bumped out an extra beat. She'd never worn an orange shirt.

Didn't mean she didn't have one. He lifted the shirt from the top of the numbered cubby and stared at the brightly colored fox. It wore a big poodley skirt and seemed to be dancing. Under the animal, it read FOX TROT in bright blue letters.

He smiled. This was the one. Now he just needed a pair of funky glasses to go with it. After deeming all the reading glasses at the department store too ordinary, he paid for the T-shirt and left.

In the truck, with the air conditioner blowing, he tried to think of where he could find the kind of glasses he needed. Inspiration struck him, and he said, "All right, Sully. Are you ready for a ride?"

By the time he'd secured all the things he needed to go next door and make his apology for breaking things off so prematurely, without giving Wren much of a chance to explain herself, it was too late to do such things.

So he endured a sleepless night with the scent of roses in his nostrils and the hope that he could catch her in the morning before she left for work.

The sun had barely started to paint the countryside with golden light when he stood on her doorstep, each hand holding multiple things, making it impossible for him to ring the doorbell or knock.

He was just about to set down the bag he'd lovingly placed the T-shirt in when Wren opened the door.

Tate sucked in a breath, unable to speak now that he was finally face-to-face with her. She stared at him, then let her gaze slide down his chest to his hands, where he held a vase of red roses in one hand, with a bakery bag hooked to his pinky finger, and the gift bag with her presents in the other. That hand also held the notebook paper he'd scrawled his budget on the previous evening.

She cocked one hip, her mouth twitching like she wanted to smile but didn't at the same time. "Good morning, Tate," she said.

The sound of her voice launched him into action, and he thrust the flowers toward her. "I got these for you, and I'm here to apologize."

She did allow herself that smile now, and she took the vase and lifted the petals to her nose, where she took a deep breath. "The last man who brought me roses ended up breaking my heart." Wren stepped back, a clear invitation for him to come in off the porch, and pushed up her black glasses frames.

Tate entered, taking in the usual clutter. Wren's usual T-shirt, this one green with bright gold coins all over it, and a pair of white shorts. She didn't wear shoes, and she moved behind him to put the roses in a tiny bare spot on the kitchen island.

"I'm not going to break your heart," Tate said, his face toward the fancy tile on her kitchen floor. "At least, I hope not."

"What's in the bag?"

"Which one?"

She pointed to the bakery bag. "Baklava," he said. "See, I went out last night to get everything, and I remembered you saying that your grandmother was a big fan. I know it's not a breakfast item, but—"

Wren put her forefinger on his lips, effectively silencing him and shooting hot sparks through his whole face.

"I'm sure it's delicious." She took the bag and extracted the treat. "I'll save it for tonight."

"And I got you a couple of things." He placed the bag on top of a stack of magazines, nearly fisting the paper he still held.

"Should I open it?"

"Sure."

She took the tissue paper out of the bag and withdrew the pair of bright blue frames he'd found in the drug store in Vernal, her eyes darting back to his.

"They have no prescription," he said. "I thought you'd maybe like to change up your look from time to time."

She removed the black frames and slid the blue ones onto her nose. When she looked at him again, it was with unwavering faith and tears in her eyes. She didn't blink or look away, and regret lanced through Tate.

"I'm so sorry," he whispered. "I didn't even give you a chance to explain anything, and—"

Wren's tears splashed her cheeks, but she made no move to wipe them. Tate hated seeing her so distraught and knowing he was the cause of it. His own emotion balled up and threatened to choke him.

Wren finally tore her gaze from his and pulled out the T-shirt. Her giggle made him want to smile, want to live again, and in that single moment, he knew he was in love with Wren Fuller.

She held the fox up to her body. "Thank you. This is fantastic." Laying the shirt on the other stuff already on the counter, she looked at him again. "And that?" She nodded to his fist and the paper he clenched there.

"This is...this is why I freaked out and broke up with you."

She backed up against the table and folded her arms. "So I probably don't want to see it."

"We need to talk about it." He advanced toward her and flattened the paper against his chest before extending it toward her. "It's what I make in a month. I did all these numbers for expenses and budgets, and I don't think—" His voice broke, but he forged onward anyway. "I don't think I can support you the way you're used to being taken care of. But I'm absolutely miserable without you."

Wren didn't so much as twitch toward the paper. "I don't care about money."

Tate wanted to scoff, but he held it back. "Good, because I'm in love with you, and I'm tired of going up to visit Octagon by myself. Tired of sitting at church by myself. Tired of trying to sleep at night without having kissed you—"

She silenced him this time by covering his mouth with hers. And all the negativity that had been ballooning inside Tate's chest since he'd made the budget that showed they'd barely have enough to buy coffee and cream to go with it simply disappeared.

CHAPTER 15

Wren let herself fly on the high that was kissing Tate after he'd said he was in love with her. And with the new glasses, and the cute fox shirt, and the roses, she didn't care what that paper said.

"I love you, too," she whispered against his lips, glad when his arms came around her and held her against him while he kissed her deeper. He pulled back a moment later, and she tucked herself against his chest.

"The budget only has my income in it," he said. "But if you worked too, we'll probably be okay." He inched away from her, and she wished he didn't want to talk about this right now. She just wanted to bask in the woodsy smell of him and taste his lips again.

"And just so you know, you probably make more than I do. So if you want to have kids, and we do, I'm not stuck on the traditional gender roles."

She smiled at his serious nature, the way he talked about having a family with her so casually. "So you'll be Mister Mom while I answer phones and arrange schedules?"

"You run the whole company," he said. "That's a lot more than answering phones."

She blinked at him, not quite sure how he knew what her job entailed. It wasn't a particularly hard job—her dad still managed all the cash flow—but yes, it was more than answering phones.

"I know how to do laundry, and I'm great with dishes," Tate said.

"I've seen your place," Wren said. "I know what a neat freak you are." She gestured to the mess surrounding them. "This is who I am."

She caught the slight grimace as Tate took in the cluttered kitchen. "I know who you are, Wren."

"I started volunteering at the library," she said.

His eyebrows lifted, and she said, "Yeah. I felt like I needed to get outside myself. Focus on serving others for a while. It's been...." She couldn't think of the right word to describe her service at the library. While she was there, she didn't have to think about her own problems. She realized just how good the things in her life were. She felt liberated every time she stepped through the door and into the brown brick building on Main Street.

"Nice," she finished.

"Why'd you start doing that?" he asked.

"I realized how selfish I am."

"Wren—"

"No, it's true. I have had an easy life, handed almost everything I have. I've never wondered if I'd have a job, or how I'd pay for things. I work with people who have enough to hire us to do their cleaning and mow their lawns. And maybe my eyes needed to be opened to the fact that not everyone in this town is as fortunate."

"And have you seen that?"

She nodded, that blasted emotion so close to the surface again. "I've only been doing it for a week, but yes. I've seen kids come in without shoes, and when I asked the head librarian, she said the family couldn't afford shoes."

The very idea was unfathomable to her. She had a closet full of shoes and could get a new pair whenever she wanted.

Wren took a deep breath and scanned Tate's civilian clothes. "You're not working today?"

"I am, yeah."

"Don't you need to get going?"

"You didn't even look at the budget."

"I don't care about money. We'll make it work." Wren tiptoed her fingers up the buttons on his shirt, finally looking up through her eyelashes at him. "All right, Tate?

She'd never been happier than when he simply said, "All right." He leaned his forehead down, as if praying, and Wren basked in the soft moment between them.

"Wren, I just want you to know..... If we're talking about marriage, I'm going to need time for that."

"So you don't need it done today?" She grinned at him, sure teasing him about how he'd demanded a maid the very hour he'd called would never get old.

Thankfully, he smiled too as he slowly shook his head. "Not today. I want to go a little slower this time. All right, Wren?"

She curled her fingers along the back of his neck and skated them over the short hair there, eliciting a shiver from him. "All right."

THE NEXT SUMMER

When Tate said he needed time, he wasn't kidding. Wren honestly hadn't minded—until he'd proposed. That had finally happened on Valentine's Day, and the last four months had seemed to drag by in one eternal block of time.

"Did Berlin bring the flowers?" she asked as her mom bustled into the room with a makeup kit the size of a small suitcase.

"She and Fabi are setting it all up now."

Wren nodded and turned back to the mirror where she sat. Over the course of the last year, she'd managed to grow her hair out enough to have several locks of hair twisted into roses and pinned along the nape of her neck.

She'd spent some time over the past twelve months looking at wedding magazines, following stylists and dress makers on social media, and mapping out her plan for a wedding the town of Brush Creek would never forget. Because practically everyone was coming.

Her father and brothers had been setting up tables and chairs for two days. Jazzy and Fabi had tied the bright yellow and pink bows to the backs of the chairs, and Berlin had secured tablecloths to all thirty-one tables situated in the back yard.

"Let me in here." Her mom set the makeup kit on the vanity in front of her, and Wren scooted back. Being the first Fuller sister to get married was a huge to-do for her mom, and Wren had counseled with her for many hours over how to make this a grand affair without going over the top.

She'd told her parents why Tate had backed off early in their relationship, and they'd agreed to do everything they could for as little money as possible. Thus, everyone in the family was pitching in to help, and the most expensive item in the budget had been the food.

"Granny Ebony will finish up the dress in no time," her mom said.

Wren nodded, though she automatically pressed her lips together in worry. She could practically hear the sewing machine humming as her grandmother hurried to finish the last-minute alterations on the homemade wedding dress she'd been working on for months.

Of course she couldn't. The sewing room was in the basement, and she and her mother were in her old bedroom, which had been turned into the bride's room. She was getting married right here in her parent's back yard, by Pastor Peters and with her family and friends in attendance.

Tears sprang to her eyes and her mother swept them away. "It's going to be a wonderful day," she said kindly. "Nothing to cry about."

Wren gave a short burst of a nod and pulled back on her emotions. She was just so happy. "Is this what it was like when you married Dad?" she asked.

Her mom began pulling out pots of makeup and consulting the list she'd made for blush colors and eye shadow combinations. "Yes, dear." A smile crossed her mother's face. "It was the happiest day of my life. We're still very happy together." She picked up a brush. "You and Tate will be too."

Wren closed her eyes as her mother began sweeping foundation onto her face. "I know, Mom." And she did know. She and Tate had attended twelve weeks of counseling together, provided by the Marines for their retirees and their families. Though she and Tate weren't quite a family yet, he'd asked her to go with him.

She'd learned a lot about him just by spending time with him over the months, but the counseling sessions revealed a deeper man. One who hurt deeply. One who learned from that hurt. One who used it to drive himself to be better. She'd fallen in love with him over and over again as they completed the counseling courses.

"Did everything go okay with the paperwork yesterday?" her mother asked. "You never said."

"Mm hm." Wren kept her eyes shut as her mom switched to a powder and a softer, wider makeup brush. "And I hired Pat and Brennan to move my stuff next door while Tate and I are gone."

"Do you know who bought your cottage?"

Wren had never imagined that she and Tate would live in her house. After all, he owned his and not having a mortgage payment—not to mention a bigger space—made more sense than living in the cottage, no matter how much she loved it.

"A young couple," she said. "I think their name was Grigsby."

"Huh. Don't know that name."

Wren said nothing. Brush Creek was growing, and soon it would be impossible for her mother, despite her lifelong habitation in the town, to know everyone.

"He's a chemistry teacher at the high school," Wren said. "Been there a year, I think."

"Hmm." Her mother worked in silence after that, and Wren stayed as still as possible. It seemed like only minutes later that her mom announced, "All right, dear. Take a look."

Wren opened her eyes, taking a few seconds for her eyes to focus. The beautiful woman staring back at her in the mirror looked mature, wise, and ready to marry the love of her life.

"You'll have to do the mascara," her mom said. "I'm no good at that."

"But brilliant at everything else." Wren stood and embraced her mom. "Thanks, Mom." She reached for the tube of mascara but only had one eye done when the door opened and Granny Ebony came through, both arms straight out in front of her to support the wedding dress.

"Finished," she said, positively beaming.

Her mother moved to help her, but all Wren could do was watch. Her other grandma came in too, and Wren's gratitude was so overwhelming she sank back into the chair where she'd been sitting.

Sometimes her family annoyed her. Sometimes they were loud and obnoxious. Sometimes she had to deal with problems they caused through no fault of hers.

But she loved them. And they loved her. They had shown her for years how to be a family, how to love unconditionally, and how to make things work even when they weren't perfect.

As she'd continued to volunteer at the library, Wren had learned a lot of the same lessons. How to love people who were different from her. How to put someone else's needs above hers. How to get along with people even when she didn't agree with them.

She closed her eyes again and said a prayer. *Dear Lord, thank you for the experiences of the past year. Thank you for transforming me into the person who can love and support*

Tate. Help us to love unconditionally, work through things that aren't perfect, and put each other first.

"Wren," her mom said, jolting her out of her private moment.

With her eyes open, she added *And thank you.*

"People are starting to arrive." Her mom nodded toward her grandmother, who stood at the window. "Finish up your makeup so we can get you dressed."

CHAPTER 17

Tate stared at himself in the mirror, his heartbeat pulsing in the vein in his neck. Though he was sheltered from the events happening just outside the door and down the hall, he was aware of the increased energy in the air.

"Almost time," his father said.

Tate ran his fingers down the buttons on his jacket, though they were all in place. He adjusted his belt a hair to the right.

"You ready?" His dad's presence had calmed him, and it had been fun to introduce him and his girlfriend, whom he'd brought with him from Shiloh Ridge, to the Fullers. He'd called them all the wrong name at least once, and Tate didn't feel so bad for taking several weeks to get them all straight.

"Yes." He turned from the mirror without a trace of doubt in his voice or his system. He was ready. It may have taken him a while to get to the ready point, but he'd reached it. That was all that mattered.

A knock sounded on the door, and his dad got up to answer it. Cory, a dark-haired cop who was now Tate's partner entered. He wore his full police uniform too, and Tate smiled at him.

"Are they ready?"

"Guests are in place." Cory scanned him. "I should've joined the Marines. That's way better than this." He gestured to his getup.

"None of it breathes," Tate said. He took his hat from his dad and tucked it under his arm so he could put on his gloves.

"I've already got Sully at my house," Cory said. "And I'll check on the house every couple of days, just to make sure the sprinklers haven't flooded or something."

Tate nodded, grateful this past year had provided him with new friends and new opportunities to grow. Some of it may not have been pleasant, but he felt more like the person he wanted to be. Less angry. Less depressed. More like someone who could actually be a good husband for someone like Wren.

"All right, then," Cory said. "We better go. They don't want you seeing Wren before the ceremony."

"Isn't she all the way upstairs?" Tate positioned his hat on his head, disliking the limited sight it created. He wanted to see everything and everyone—especially Wren as she walked toward him to become his wife.

"Yes, but word is she's ready to start. So let's go."

Cory opened the door and stepped into the hall. Tate started to follow him, pausing in front of his father.

"Do I look ready to get married?" he asked.

His dad wore such pride on his face. Such love. "You sure do." He hugged him, and a rush of gratitude for his dad filled him. No, his family wasn't huge. Or traditional. But they still stuck together and loved each other.

Tate stepped back and tugged on the bottom of his jacket to get it back in place. His legs moved him outside, and he drank in the splendor of the Fuller's back yard. Dozens of tables had been set up for the meal that would follow the ceremony, and the bright colors Wren had wanted complemented the blue sky and green grass beautifully.

Everyone stood as he entered the yard and walked down the aisle Wren soon would too. Tate blinked back his emotion as he saw the entire police force there, including Dahlia, who'd stayed in contact once she'd been appointed one of the joint detectives. They all saluted him, and Tate stopped and clicked his heels together. He saluted them back and continued toward the pastor at the end of the aisle.

A hush had fallen over the yard, but once he was in place, people began whispering again. Tate turned back the way he'd come, his eyes trained on the French doors so he wouldn't miss a moment of watching Wren.

She hadn't told him anything about her dress, other

than her grandmother was making it. He couldn't wait to see her in it, see if she chose to wear the glasses she didn't need or not, see what magic her old high school friend at the salon had done with her hair.

"No matter what it is," she'd told him. "It will be a miracle if it looks good."

Tate thought her hair always looked good, but she'd just rolled her eyes when he'd said that.

Her two grandmothers came out first, and one of them paused to start the wedding march on the CD player. Speakers had been set in the crowd, so everyone could hear the music as the bridal party moved down the aisle.

Finally, only Wren stood opposite of him, wearing miles and miles of lace. She held a bouquet of pink and yellow roses and a tiny flower crown with delicate white flowers in it. Her face beamed with light and happiness that mirrored the way Tate felt every time he looked at her.

His breath caught in his chest, and he couldn't get a full breath until she reached him, passed her bouquet to her mother, and laced her arm through his.

"Wow," she whispered, a giggle escaping her mouth as he led her around the altar so they were facing their families and friends. "Don't you look handsome and regal?"

"Oh yeah?"

She reached over and fiddled with a button on his

jacket, a flirty, sexy thing to do right in front of everyone.

"Well, you look beautiful," he whispered, pressing his lips to her temple and facing the pastor. He was aware of the sea of faces beyond Pastor Peters, but he didn't allow himself to get lost in them.

He focused on the feel of Wren's body next to his, and the words Pastor Peters said.

"When we join together in marriage, each partner must leave behind something of themselves and become one." He smiled at them and began to recite a poem. He counseled them to talk to each other always, and include the Lord in their lives and marriage.

Finally, he said, "Well, I think we need to get this wedding done, before this Marine melts."

The crowd twittered, Tate along with them. He turned toward Wren and lost himself in the beauty of her gentle soul, in the fact that someone as wonderful as her could fall in love with him. He marveled that thirteen months ago, he'd come to Brush Creek to build a new life—and he'd actually done it.

He'd been so lost, so lonely, so low. Somehow he'd replaced that man with the one standing in the gardens today—and he'd never been happier.

"You may kiss your bride."

Tate startled, realizing he'd missed part of the vows as he gazed at Wren. She smiled up at him, and he swept his hat off his head and swooped her closer so he could kiss her.

And though every kiss with Wren was filled with magic, this first one with her as his wife was definitely the sweetest.

Read on for a sneak peek of THE FIREFIGHTER'S FIANCÉ, available now.

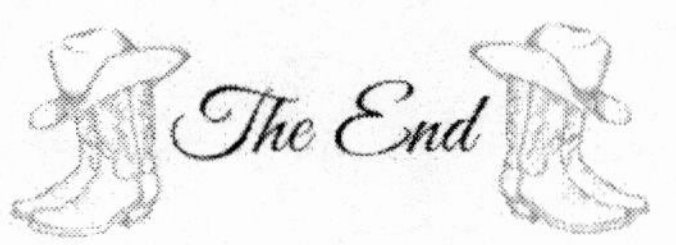
The End

SNEAK PEEK! THE FIREFIGHTER'S FIANCÉ
CHAPTER ONE

Cora Wesley tipped her head back, the bottom of her ponytail brushing down her back as she laughed. The atmosphere in the karaoke bar vibrated with energy, with sound waves from the stage, with chatter and laughter and friendship.

She quieted, realizing she was the only woman at the table of firefighters. She'd been in Brush Creek for a year and had gotten used to the nearly female-free department, but she knew she sometimes stuck out like that one Christmas light that kept blinking when it was supposed to stay steady.

She picked up her strawberry lemonade and licked the sugary rim while the firefighter currently telling jokes started in on another one. A pause of silence in the music behind her alerted her to the change in singers, and the next song began. A horrible, nasally voice started on the lyrics, causing her to twist to see what poor soul had decided to take the mic and try to sing an Adele song—clearly out of her vocal range.

Not that Cora was a good singer by any stretch of the imagination. But she knew her limits and wouldn't embarrass herself on purpose. The redhead on stage glanced around nervously, her eyes landing on a table of women a couple over from Cora and her squad of bulky firefighters. All the women had been eyeing their table the entire evening, and while none of her firemen buddies had made a move, they'd all noticed.

The amount of flexing and loud laughter testified of that. Cora couldn't help joining in. She liked her friends at Station House Two, and if she didn't come out on Friday nights with them, she'd be excluded in their camaraderie by more than her gender.

Plus, she liked going out with them. There were only so many hours in a day that she could run and lift weights. She drained the last of her lemonade, vowing not to order another. She wasn't big by any stretch of the imagination, but she needed to meet certain physical standards to apply for the interagency hotshot crews. She wanted the Great Basin crew, so she could stay in Utah, Idaho, and Nevada. But Cora would take any crew that would take her.

So with a determination to put in another fifty pushups after she returned to her solitary, quite apartment that night, she tuned back in to Jorge's joke about a duck and why he couldn't cross the road.

As the other men broke into another round of

raucous laughter, her phone blinked and vibrated the table in front of her. She swiped it into her lap to read her sister's text. Helene was already married and settled in Vernal, where Cora's parents lived. Where she'd been raised.

Mom wants to know if you're coming to the family anniversary party.

Cora's stomach twisted and her mouth felt sour—and not because of the lemonade she'd drunk. The family anniversary party was a celebration of the day the Wesley family had begun—the day her parents had gotten married forty years ago.

She started thumbing out a response when Helene added *It's a big one. Forty years.*

Cora erased her rejection to her older sister. She couldn't miss the forty-year anniversary. Thirty-nine, sure. Forty-one, definitely. But not this one.

She sighed, her mind far from the party atmosphere now. The waitress approached their table, and her friends ordered more sodas, but Cora waved her hand. Someone asked her something, but her thoughts lingered on what family functions used to be like for her. They were so much easier when she had someone to attend them with.

"Do you want to add your name to the list?" Charlie, the man seated next to her, asked.

"Yeah, sure," she said distractedly, an idea churning in her head now. If she could take someone to the family anniversary party, things would be easier for everyone. No one knew what to say to her now, without Brandt on her arm. She glanced at the six men she spent most of her life with. Maybe one of them....

She banished the thought before it could truly take root. Her ex, Brandt, had been a firefighter, and she wasn't interested in getting involved with another one. They were great friends. Great boyfriends. Not great husbands, at least in her experience.

She knew she was being totally unfair. There were several married firefighters and their wives seemed happy enough. *It was just a bad match*, she told herself, signaling for another lemonade despite her promise to herself.

Well? Are you coming?

Helene wouldn't be put off, and if Cora didn't answer her, she'd call. So Cora picked up her phone and said, *Yes, I'll be there.*

Bringing anyone?

At that moment, Charlie plucked her phone from her hand. "You're missing out," he said, placing it face-down on the table on his left, out of her reach.

"It's my sister," she said, panic rearing in her chest now.

"Kent asked what song you're singing." Charlie nodded to the man sitting next to Cora on her other side.

Confusion needled her. "Singing?" She scoffed. "I'm not singing." Sure, she'd come to the karaoke bar, but she never sang.

"You told Charlie to tell Sissy to put you on the list," Kent said. "I thought it was weird." He nodded toward the phone. "Let me see that."

Cora made a lunge for her device as Charlie passed it over to him, both of them chuckling. She'd learned in the first day at the Brush Creek Fire Department not to keep anything sensitive on her phone. They got passed around like sticks of gum, and she sometimes texted her mates from someone else's phone.

"It's nothing," she said.

"Family anniversary party," Kent read, his dark eyes squinting in concentration. A whistle followed. "Wow, forty years." He handed the phone back to her. "Are you going with anyone?"

No one in Brush Creek knew she'd been married before, and she wanted to keep it that way. She'd dated at least a dozen men in the year she'd been in town. Dated wasn't really the right word. She went to dinner with a guy and then didn't call him back. Or hung out with a man for a couple of weeks before settling into friend territory.

She'd met a few men that stirred her interest, but her goal of landing on a hotshot crew always kept her focus away from starting something serious. She simply wasn't interested in serious.

"I don't know." Cora sighed out her answer. She looked at Kent and then Charlie, wondering if she could ask one of them to go with her. Kent probably would.

He'd been one she'd eaten burgers with and then brushed off.

Kent flipped her ponytail like an annoying older brother. "Still no boyfriend, then?"

Cora snorted, all the answer that question required.

The conversation at the table quieted, and Cora glanced around, wondering if her disgust at Kent's question had really been that loud.

"Go on, then," Jorge said, folding his giant arms and making his biceps bulge. It was a miracle the women a couple of tables over didn't faint at the sight.

"Go on where?" Cora asked, reaching for her refilled glass of lemonade.

"They just called your name." He nodded toward the stage, and Cora whipped her attention behind her so fast her neck sent a shock of pain down her spine.

Kent nudged her out of her seat and Charlie pushed her toward the steps amidst her protests. Along the way, she passed a table of men, all of them with sandy hair and light eyes. They smiled at her in what she was sure was meant to be encouragement.

She knew who they were; everyone knew the Fullers. But she didn't know any of the men by name, only reputation, and when one nodded at her, his grin fading to the natural strong set of his jaw, she paused.

All noise fell away, leaving just a silent conduit from her to this handsome Fuller man seated furthest from her.

Somehow, her feet took her up the steps to the

stage, and it seemed like everyone in the bar had suddenly run out of things to say to one another. With sixty pairs of eyes on her, she gripped the mic and pointed to the song she wanted to sing.

The music started, a slow ballad of a childhood song she'd grown up belting out with her brother and sister. She closed her eyes just before starting on the first line, really losing herself to the moment and hoping with everything in her that she didn't make a complete fool of herself.

"Lying in my bed, I hear the clock tick and think of you."

She opened her eyes, her gaze locking onto the man watching her intently now. One of his brothers elbowed him, but he didn't look away from her.

Cora didn't need to look at the screen to keep signing. She belted out the chorus with accuracy, putting on a good show as she became aware of her firefighter crew yelping and whooping their encouragement.

But she absolutely couldn't look away from the mystery man who'd captured her attention in a single moment of time.

He got up and went over to the table where she'd been sitting with her back to him, leaning down to say something to Charlie. Kent joined the conversation, and Cora's blood boiled because no doubt they were talking about her.

"Time after time," she sang into the mic. "Time after time." One last big breath, and she ended with another,

"Time after time," in the best breathy Cyndi Lauper voice she could muster. The 80s music faded, leaving only her, alone on the stage in her tight black jeans and flowy black tank top, her hand dropping to her side as if the mic were too heavy to hold up for another moment.

She handed it to Sissy and stumbled toward the steps, at the bottom of which Kent and Charlie were now clapping. Before she'd even gotten both feet on solid ground, Kent pushed her toward the man who'd singlehandedly gotten her pulse racing and said, "Here's your next date, Cora."

She fumbled into him, her hands landing solidly on his chest. His very solid, wide chest.

Cora swallowed, righted herself, and glared at Kent. "I'm not looking for a date."

"Sure you are," Charlie said. "To your parent's party."

Humiliation crept up Cora's back and down her arms. "You guys—no." She met the Fuller man's eyes and nearly drowned in the beautiful depths of them. "No offense," she managed to squeak out.

My, he was handsome. Tall. With loads of sandy hair that would surely glide right through her fingers like silk. And those hazel eyes that looked dark as chocolate in this dim bar lighting.

"I'm Brennan Fuller," he said, extending his hand toward her to shake. "I don't think we've met."

That same floaty feeling that had happened the first time they'd looked at one another happened again.

Kent's voice faded. Charlie's body behind her, trapping her close to Brennan, disappeared.

There was just this Brennan Fuller man wearing half a coy smile, and Cora. The two of them breathed in and out together, and Cora found herself saying, "I'm Cora Wesley. How do you feel about stuffy anniversary parties with dozens of married people?"

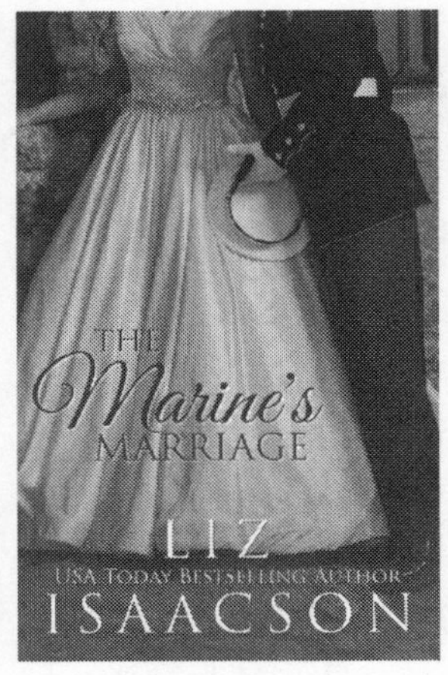

The Marine's Marriage (Book 1): Tate Benson can't believe he's come to Nowhere, Utah, to fix up a house that hasn't been inhabited in years. But he has. Because he's retired from the Marines and looking to start a life as a police officer in small-town Brush Creek. Wren Fuller has her hands full most days running her family's company. When Tate calls and demands a maid for that morning, she decides to have the calls forwarded to her cell and go help him out. She didn't know he was moving in next door, and she's completely unprepared for his handsomeness, his kind heart, and his wounded soul.Can Tate and Wren weather a relationship when they're also next-door neighbors?

The Firefighter's Fiancé (Book 2): Cora Wesley comes to Brush Creek, hoping to get some in-the-wild firefighting training as she prepares to put in her application to be a hotshot. When she meets Brennan Fuller, the spark between them is hot and instant. As they get to know each other, her deadline is constantly looming over them, and Brennan starts to wonder if he can break ranks in the family business. He's okay mowing lawns and hanging out with his brothers, but he dreams of being able to go to college and become a landscape architect, but he's just not sure it can be done. Will Cora and Brennan be able to endure their trials to find true love?

The Trooper's Treasure (Book 3): Dawn Fuller has made some mistakes in her life, and she's not proud of the way McDermott Boyd found her off the road one day last year. She's spent a hard year wrestling with her choices and trying to fix them, glad for McDermott's acceptance and friendship. He lost his wife years ago, done his best with his daughter, and now he's ready to move on. Can McDermott help Dawn find a way past her former mistakes and down a path that leads to love, family, and happiness?

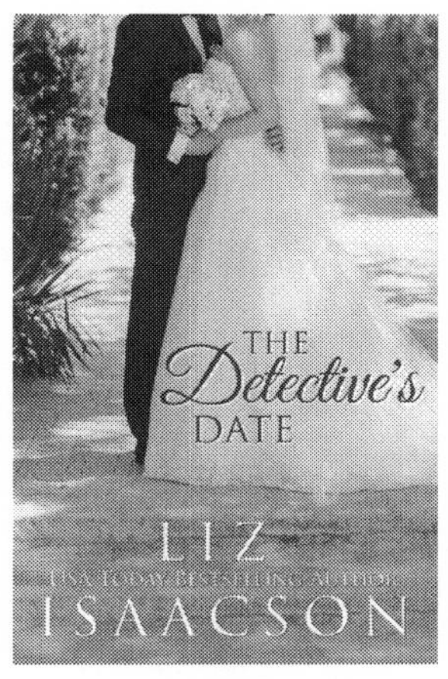

The Detective's Date (Book 4): Dahlia Reid is one of the best detectives Brush Creek and the surrounding towns has ever had. She's given up on the idea of marriage—and pleasing her mother—and has dedicated herself fully to her job. Which is great, since one of the most perplexing cases of her career has come to town. Kyler Fuller thinks he's finally ready to move past the woman who ghosted him years ago. He's cut his hair, and he's ready to start dating. Too bad every woman he's been out with is about as interesting as a lamppost—until Dahlia. He finds her beautiful, her quick wit a breath of fresh air, and her intelligence sexy. Can Kyler and Dahlia use their faith to find a way through the obstacles threatening to keep them apart?

The Paramedic's Partner (Book 5): Jazzy Fuller has always been overshadowed by her prettier, more popular twin, Fabiana. Fabi meets paramedic Max Robinson at the park and sets a date with him only to come down with the flu. So she convinces Jazzy to cut her hair and take her place on the date. And the spark between Jazzy and Max is hot and instant...if only he knew she wasn't her sister, Fabi.

Max drives the ambulance for the town of Brush Creek with is partner Ed Moon, and neither of them have been all that lucky in love. Until Max suggests to who he thinks is Fabi that they should double with Ed and Jazzy. They do, and Fabi is smitten with the steady, strong Ed Moon. As each twin falls further and further in love with their respective paramedic, it becomes obvious they'll need to come clean about the switcheroo sooner rather than later...or risk losing their hearts.

The Chief's Catch (Book 6): Berlin Fuller has struck out with the dating scene in Brush Creek more times than she cares to admit. When she makes a deal with her friends that they can choose the next man she goes out with, she didn't dream they'd pick surly Cole Fairbanks, the new Chief of Police.

His friends call him the Beast and challenge him to complete ten dates that summer or give up his bonus check. When Berlin approaches him, stuttering about the deal with her friends and claiming they don't actually have to go out, he's intrigued. As the summer passes, Cole finds himself burning both ends of the candle to keep up with his job and his new relationship. When he unleashes the Beast one time too many, Berlin will have to decide if she can tame him or if she should walk away.

BOOKS IN THE BRUSH CREEK COWBOYS ROMANCE SERIES:

Brush Creek Cowboy (Book 1): Former rodeo champion and cowboy Walker Thompson trains horses at Brush Creek Horse Ranch, where he lives a simple life in his cabin with his ten-year-old son. A widower of six years, he's worked with Tess Wagner, a widow who came to Brush Creek to escape the turmoil of her life to give her seven-year-old son a slower pace of life. But Tess's breast cancer is back...

Walker will have to decide if he'd rather spend even a short time with Tess than not have her in his life at all. Tess wants to feel God's love and power, but can she discover and accept God's will in order to find her happy ending?

The Cowboy's Challenge (Book 2): Cowboy and professional roper Justin Jackman has found solitude at Brush Creek Horse Ranch, preferring his time with the animals he trains over dating. With two failed engagements in his past, he's not really interested in getting his heart stomped on again. But when flirty and fun Renee Martin picks him up at a church ice cream bar--on a bet, no less--he finds himself more than just a little interested. His Gen-X attitudes are attractive to her; her Millennial behaviors drive him nuts. Can Justin look past their differences and take a chance on another engagement?

A Cowboy's Proposal (Book 3): Ted Caldwell has been a retired bronc rider for years, and he thought he was perfectly happy training horses to buck at Brush Creek Ranch. He was wrong. When he meets April Nox, who comes to the ranch to hide her pregnancy from all her friends back in Jackson Hole, Ted realizes he has a huge family-shaped hole in his life. April is embarrassed, heartbroken, and trying to find her extinguished faith. She's never ridden a horse and wants nothing to do with a cowboy ever again. Can Ted and April create a family of happiness and love from a tragedy?

A New Family for the Cowboy (Book 4): Blake Gibbons oversees all the agriculture at Brush Creek Horse Ranch, sometimes moonlighting as a general contractor. When he meets Erin Shields, new in town, at her aunt's bakery, he's instantly smitten. Erin moved to Brush Creek after a divorce that left

her penniless, homeless, and a single mother of three children under age eight. She's nowhere near ready to start dating again, but the longer Blake hangs around the bakery, the more she starts to like him. Can Blake and Erin find a way to blend their lifestyles and become a family?

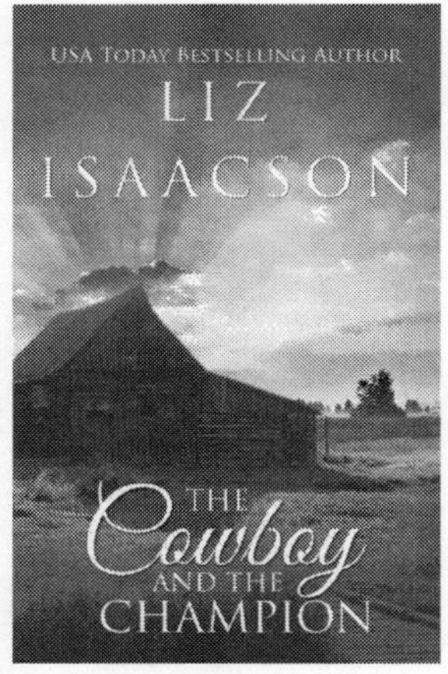

The Cowboy and the Champion (Book 5): Emmett Graves has always had a positive outlook on life. He adores training horses to become barrel racing champions during the day and cuddling with his cat at night. Fresh off her professional rodeo retirement, Molly Brady comes to Brush Creek Horse Ranch as Emmett's protege. He's not thrilled, and she's allergic to cats. Oh, and she'd like to stay cowboy-free, thank you very much. But Emmett's about as cowboy as they come.... Can Emmett and Molly work together without falling in love?

Schooled by the Cowboy (Book 6): Grant Ford spends his days training cattle—when he's not camped out at the elementary school hoping to catch a glimpse of his ex-girlfriend. When principal Shannon Sharpe confronts him and asks him to stay away from the school, the spark between them is instant and hot. Shannon's expecting a transfer very soon, but she also needs a summer outdoor coordinator—and Grant fits the bill. Just because he's handsome and everything Shannon's ever wanted in a cowboy husband means nothing. Will Grant and Shannon be able to survive the summer or will the Utah heat be too much for them to handle?

BOOKS IN THE SEVEN SONS RANCH IN THREE RIVERS ROMANCE SERIES

Rhett's Make-Believe Marriage (Book 1): She needs a husband to be credible as a matchmaker. He wants to help a neighbor. Will their fake marriage take them out of the friend zone?

Tripp's Trivial Tie (Book 2): She needs a husband to keep her son. He's wanted to take their relationship to the next level, but she's always pushing him away. Will their trivial tie take them all the way to happily-ever-after?

Liam's Invented I-Do (Book 3): She needs a husband to be credible as a matchmaker. He wants to help a neighbor. Will their fake marriage take them out of the friend zone?

Jeremiah's Bogus Bride (Book 4): He wants to prove to his brothers that he's not broken. She just wants him. Will a fake marriage heal him or push her further away?

Wyatt's Pretend Pledge (Book 5): To get her inheritance, she needs a husband. He's wanted to fly with her for ages. Can their pretend pledge turn into something real?

Skyler's Wanna-Be Wife (Book 6): She needs a new last name to stay in school. He's willing to help a fellow student. Can this wanna-be wife show the playboy that some things should be taken seriously?

Micah's Mock Matrimony (Book 7): They were just actors in a play. The marriage was just for the crowd – until a clerical error results in a legal marriage. Can these two neighbors negotiate this new ground between them and achieve new roles in each other's lives?

BOOKS IN THE CHRISTMAS IN CORAL CANYON ROMANCE SERIES

Her Cowboy Billionaire Best Friend (Book 1): Graham Whittaker returns to Coral Canyon a few days after Christmas—after the death of his father. He takes over the energy company his dad built from the ground up and buys a high-end lodge to live in—only a mile from the home of his once-best friend, Laney McAllister. They were best friends once, but Laney's always entertained feelings for him, and spending so much time with him while they make Christmas memories puts her heart in danger of getting broken again...

Her Cowboy Billionaire Boss (Book 2): Since the death of his wife a few years ago, Eli Whittaker has been running from one job to another, unable to find somewhere for him and his son to settle. Meg Palmer is Stockton's nanny, and she comes with her boss, Eli, to the lodge, her long-time crush on the man no different in Wyoming than it was on the beach. When she confesses her feelings for him and gets nothing in return, she's crushed, embarrassed, and unsure if she can stay in Coral Canyon for Christmas. Then Eli starts to show some feelings for her too...

Her Cowboy Billionaire Boyfriend (Book 3): Andrew Whittaker is the public face for the Whittaker Brothers' family energy company, and with his older brother's robot about to be announced, he needs a press secretary to help him get everything ready and tour the state to make the announcements. When he's hit by a protest sign being carried by the company's biggest opponent, Rebecca Collings, he learns with a few clicks that she has the background they need. He offers her the job of press secretary when she thought she was going to be arrested, and not only because the spark between them in so hot Andrew can't see straight.

Can Becca and Andrew work together and keep their relationship a secret? Or will hearts break in this classic romance retelling reminiscent of *Two Weeks Notice*?

Her Cowboy Billionaire Bodyguard (Book 4): Beau Whittaker has watched his brothers find love one by one, but every attempt he's made has ended in disaster. Lily Everett has been in the spotlight since childhood and has half a dozen platinum records with her two sisters. She's taking a break from the brutal music industry and hiding out in Wyoming while her ex-husband continues to cause trouble for her. When she hears of Beau Whittaker and what he offers his clients, she wants to meet him. Beau is instantly attracted to Lily, but he tried a relationship with his last client that left a scar that still hasn't healed...

Can Lily use the spirit of Christmas to discover what matters most? Will Beau open his heart to the possibility of love with someone so different from him?

Her Cowboy Billionaire Bull Rider (Book 5): Todd Christopherson has just retired from the professional rodeo circuit and returned to his hometown of Coral Canyon. Problem is, he's got no family there anymore, no land, and no job. Not that he needs a job--he's got plenty of money from his illustrious career riding bulls.

Then Todd gets thrown during a routine horseback ride up the canyon, and his only support as he recovers physically is the beautiful Violet Everett. She's no nurse, but she does the best she can for the handsome cowboy. **Will she lose her heart to the billionaire bull rider? Can Todd trust that God led him to Coral Canyon...and Vi?**

Her Cowboy Billionaire Bachelor (Book 6): Rose Everett isn't sure what to do with her life now that her country music career is on hold. After all, with both of her sisters in Coral Canyon, and one about to have a baby, they're not making albums anymore.

Liam Murphy has been working for Doctors Without Borders, but he's back in the US now, and looking to start a new clinic in Coral Canyon, where he spent his summers.

When Rose wins a date with Liam in a bachelor auction, their relationship blooms and grows quickly. **Can Liam and Rose find a solution to their problems that doesn't involve one of them leaving Coral Canyon with a broken heart?**

Her Cowboy Billionaire Blind Date (Book 7): Her sons want her to be happy, but she's too old to be set up on a blind date...isn't she?

Amanda Whittaker has been looking for a second chance at love since the death of her husband several years ago. Finley Barber is a cowboy in every sense of the word. Born and raised on a racehorse farm in Kentucky, he's since moved to Dog Valley and started his own breeding stable for champion horses. He hasn't dated in years, and everything about Amanda makes him nervous.

Will Amanda take the leap of faith required to be with Finn? Or will he become just another boyfriend who doesn't make the cut?

Her Cowboy Billionaire Best Man (Book 8): When Celia Abbott-Armstrong runs into a gorgeous cowboy at her best friend's wedding, she decides she's ready to start dating again.

But the cowboy is Zach Zuckerman, and the Zuckermans and Abbotts have been at war for generations.

Can Zach and Celia find a way to reconcile their family's differences so they can have a future together?

BOOKS IN THE LAST CHANCE RANCH ROMANCE SERIES

Her Last First Kiss (Book 1): A cowgirl down on her luck hires a man who's good with horses and under the hood of a car. Can Hudson fine tune Scarlett's heart as they work together? Or will things backfire and make everything worse at Last Chance Ranch?

Her Last Billionaire Boyfriend (Book 2): A billionaire cowboy without a home meets a woman who secretly makes food videos to pay her debts...Can Carson and Adele do more than fight in the kitchens at Last Chance Ranch?

Her Last Make-Believe Marriage (Book 3): A female carpenter needs a husband just for a few days... Can Jeri and Sawyer navigate the minefield of a pretend marriage before their feelings become real?

Her Last Second Chance (Book 4): An Army cowboy, the woman he dated years ago, and their last chance at Last Chance Ranch... Can Dave and Sissy put aside hurt feelings and make their second chance romance work?

Her Last Secret Sweetheart (Book 5): A former dairy farmer and the marketing director on the ranch have to work together to make the cow cuddling program a success. But can Karla let Cache into her life? Or will she keep all her secrets from him - and keep *him* a secret too?

Her Last Cowboy Christmas (Book 6): She's tired of having her heart broken by cowboys. He waited too long to ask her out. Can Lance fix things quickly, or will Amber leave Last Chance Ranch before he can tell her how he feels?

BOOKS IN THE GRAPE SEED FALLS ROMANCE SERIES:

Choosing the Cowboy (Book 1): With financial trouble and personal issues around every corner, can Maggie Duffin and Chase Carver rely on their faith to find their happily-ever-after?

A spinoff from the #1 best-selling Three Rivers Ranch Romance novels, also by USA Today bestselling author Liz Isaacson.

Craving the Cowboy (Book 2): Dwayne Carver is set to inherit his family's ranch in the heart of Texas Hill Country, and in order to keep up with his ranch duties and fulfill his dreams of owning a horse farm, he hires top trainer Felicity Lightburne. They get along great, and she can envision herself on this new farm—at least until her mother falls ill and she has to return to help her. Can Dwayne and Felicity work through their differences to find their happily-ever-after?

Charming the Cowboy (Book 3): Third grade teacher Heather Carver has had her eye on Levi Rhodes for a couple of years now, but he seems to be blind to her attempts to charm him. When she breaks her arm while on his horse ranch, Heather infiltrates Levi's life in ways he's never thought of, and his strict anti-female stance slips. Will Heather heal his emotional scars and he care for her physical ones so they can have a real relationship?

Courting the Cowboy (Book 4): Frustrated with the cowboy-only dating scene in Grape Seed Falls, May Sotheby joins TexasFaithful.-com, hoping to find her soul mate without having to relocate--or deal with cowboy hats and boots. She has no idea that Kurt Pemberton, foreman at Grape Seed Ranch, is the man she starts communicating with... Will May be able to follow her heart and get Kurt to forgive her so they can be together?

Claiming the Cowboy, Royal Brothers Book 1 (Grape Seed Falls Romance Book 5): Unwilling to be tied down, farrier Robin Cook has managed to pack her entire life into a two-hundred-and-eighty square-foot house, and that includes her Yorkie. Cowboy and co-foreman, Shane Royal has had his heart set on Robin for three years, even though she flat-out turned him down the last time he asked her to dinner. But she's back at Grape Seed Ranch for five weeks as she works her horse-shoeing magic, and he's still interested, despite a bitter life lesson that left a bad taste for marriage in his mouth.

Robin's interested in him too. But can she find room for Shane in her tiny house--and can he take a chance on her with his tired heart?

Catching the Cowboy, Royal Brothers Book 2 (Grape Seed Falls Romance Book 6): Dylan Royal is good at two things: whistling and caring for cattle. When his cows are being attacked by an unknown wild animal, he calls Texas Parks & Wildlife for help. He wasn't expecting a beautiful mammologist to show up, all flirty and fun and everything Dylan didn't know he wanted in his life.

Hazel Brewster has gone on more first dates than anyone in Grape Seed Falls, and she thinks maybe Dylan deserves a second... Can they find their way through wild animals, huge life changes, and their emotional pasts to find their forever future?

Cheering the Cowboy, Royal Brothers Book 3 (Grape Seed Falls Romance Book 7): Austin Royal loves his life on his new ranch with his brothers. But he doesn't love that Shayleigh Hatch came with the property, nor that he has to take the blame for the fact that he now owns her childhood ranch. They rarely have a conversation that doesn't leave him furious and frustrated--and yet he's still attracted to Shay in a strange, new way.

Shay inexplicably likes him too, which utterly confuses and angers her. As they work to make this Christmas the best the Triple Towers Ranch has ever seen, can they also navigate through their rocky relationship to smoother waters?

BOOKS IN THE STEEPLE RIDGE ROMANCE SERIES:

Her Billionaire Cowboy (Book 1): Tucker Jenkins has had enough of tall buildings, traffic, and has traded in his technology firm in New York City for Steeple Ridge Horse Farm in rural Vermont. Missy Marino has worked at the farm since she was a teen, and she's always dreamed of owning it. But her ex-husband left her with a truckload of debt, making her fantasies of owning the farm unfulfilled. Tucker didn't come to the country to find a new wife, but he supposes a woman could help him start over in Steeple Ridge. Will Tucker and Missy be able to navigate the shaky ground between them to find a new beginning?

Her Restless Cowboy (Book 2): Ben Buttars is the youngest of the four Buttars brothers who come to Steeple Ridge Farm, and he finally feels like he's landed somewhere he can make a life for himself. Reagan Cantwell is a decade older than Ben and the recreational direction for the town of Island Park. Though Ben is young, he knows what he wants—and that's Rae. Can she figure out how to put what matters most in her life—family and faith—above her job before she loses Ben?

Her Faithful Cowboy (Book 3): Sam Buttars has spent the last decade making sure he and his brothers stay together. They've been at Steeple Ridge for a while now, but with the youngest married and happy, the siren's call to return to his parents' farm in Wyoming is loud in Sam's ears. He'd just go if it weren't for beautiful Bonnie Sherman, who roped his heart the first time he saw her. Do Sam and Bonnie have the faith to find comfort in each other instead of in the people who've already passed?

Her Mistletoe Cowboy (Book 4): Logan Buttars has always been good-natured and happy-go-lucky. After watching two of his brothers settle down, he recognizes a void in his life he didn't know about. Veterinarian Layla Guyman has appreciated Logan's friendship and easy way with animals when he comes into the clinic to get the service dogs. But with his future at Steeple Ridge in the balance, she's not sure a relationship with him is worth the risk. Can she rely on her faith and employ patience to tame Logan's wild heart?

Her Patient Cowboy (Book 5): Darren Buttars is cool, collected, and quiet—and utterly devastated when his girlfriend of nine months, Farrah Irvine, breaks up with him because he wanted her to ride her horse in a parade. But Farrah doesn't ride anymore, a fact she made very clear to Darren. She returned to her childhood home with so much baggage, she doesn't know where to start with the unpacking. Darren's the only Buttars brother who isn't married, and he wants to make Island Park his permanent home—with Farrah. Can they find their way through the heartache to achieve a happily-ever-after together?

BOOKS IN THE HORSESHOE HOME RANCH ROMANCE SERIES:

Falling for Her Boss: A Horseshoe Home Ranch Romance (Book 1): Jace Lovell only has one thing left after his fiancé abandons him at the altar: his job at Horseshoe Home Ranch. Belle Edmunds is back in Gold Valley and she's desperate to build a portfolio that she can use to start her own firm in Montana. Jace isn't anywhere near forgiving his fiancé, and he's not sure he's ready for a new relationship with someone as fiery and beautiful as Belle. Can she employ her patience while he figures out how to forgive so they can find their own brand of happily-ever-after?

Falling for Her Roommate: A Horseshoe Home Ranch Romance (Book 2): Professional snowboarder Sterling Maughan has sequestered himself in his family's cabin in the exclusive mountain community above Gold Valley, Montana after a devastating fall that ended his career. Norah Watson cleans Sterling's cabin and the more time they spend together, the more Sterling is interested in all things Norah. As his body heals, so does his faith. Will Norah be able to trust Sterling so they can have a chance at true love?

Falling for His Best Friend: A Horseshoe Home Ranch Romance (Book 3): Landon Edmunds has been a cowboy his whole life. An accident five years ago ended his successful rodeo career, and now he's looking to start a horse ranch--and he's looking outside of Montana. Which would be great if God hadn't brought Megan Palmer back to Gold Valley right when Landon is looking to leave. Megan and Landon work together well, and as sparks fly, she's sure God brought her back to Gold Valley so she could find her happily ever after. Through serious discussion and prayer, can Landon and Megan find their future together?

Be sure to check out the spinoff series, the Brush Creek Brides romances after you read FALLING FOR HIS BEST FRIEND. Start with A WEDDING FOR THE WIDOWER.

Falling for His Nanny: A Horseshoe Home Ranch Romance (Book 4): Twelve years ago, Owen Carr left Gold Valley—and his long-time girlfriend—in favor of a country music career in Nashville. Married and divorced, Natalie teaches ballet at the dance studio in Gold Valley, but she never auditioned for the professional company the way she dreamed of doing. With Owen back, she realizes all the opportunities she missed out on when he left all those years ago—including a future with him. Can they mend broken bridges in order to have a second chance at love?

Falling for Her Ex's Brother: A Horseshoe Home Ranch Romance (Book 5): Caleb Chamberlain has spent the last five years recovering from a horrible breakup, his alcoholism that stemmed from it, and the car accident that left him hospitalized. He's finally on the right track in his life—until Holly Gray, his twin brother's ex-fiance mistakes him for Nathan. Holly's back in Gold Valley to get the required veterinarian hours to apply for her graduate program. When the herd at Horseshoe Home comes down with pneumonia, Caleb and Holly are forced to work together in close quarters. Holly's over Nathan, but she hasn't forgiven him—or the woman she believes broke up their relationship. Can Caleb and Holly navigate such a rough past to find their happily-ever-after?

Journey to Steeple Ridge Farm with Holly—and fall in love with the cowboys there in the Steeple Ridge Romance series! Start with STARTING OVER AT STEEPLE RIDGE.

Falling for Her Old Boyfriend: A Horseshoe Home Ranch Romance (Book 6): Ty Barker has been dancing through the last thirty years of his life--and he's suddenly realized he's alone. River Lee Whitely is back in Gold Valley with her two little girls after a divorce that's left deep scars. She has a job at Silver Creek that requires her to be able to ride a horse, and she nearly tramples Ty at her first lesson. That's just fine by him, because River Lee is the girl Ty has never gotten over. Ty realizes River Lee needs time to settle into her new job, her new home, her new life as a single parent, but going slow has never been his style. But for River Lee, can Ty take the necessary steps to keep her in his life?

Falling for His Next Door Neighbor: A Horseshoe Home Ranch Romance (Book 7): Archer Bailey has already lost one job to Emersyn Enders, so he deliberately doesn't tell her about the cowhand job up at Horseshoe Home Ranch. Emery's temporary job is ending, but her obligations to her physically disabled sister aren't. As Archer and Emery work together, its clear that the sparks flying between them aren't all from their friendly competition over a job. Will Emery and Archer be able to navigate the ranch, their close quarters, and their individual circumstances to find love this holiday season?

Falling for His Nurse: A Horseshoe Home Ranch Romance (Book 8): Cowboy Elliott Hawthorne has just lost his best friend and cabin mate to the worst thing imaginable—marriage. When his brother calls about an accident with their father, Elliott rushes down to Gold Valley from the ranch only to be met with the most beautiful woman he's ever seen. His father's new physical therapist, London Marsh, likes the handsome face and gentle spirit she sees in Elliott too. Can Elliott and London navigate difficult family situations to find a happily-ever-after?

Second Chance Ranch: A Three Rivers Ranch Romance (Book 1): After his deployment, injured and discharged Major Squire Ackerman returns to Three Rivers Ranch, wanting to forgive Kelly for ignoring him a decade ago. He'd like to provide the stable life she needs, but with old wounds opening and a ranch on the brink of financial collapse, it will take patience and faith to make their second chance possible.

Third Time's the Charm: A Three Rivers Ranch Romance (Book 2): First Lieutenant Peter Marshall has a truckload of debt and no way to provide for a family, but Chelsea helps him see past all the obstacles, all the scars. With so many unknowns, can Pete and Chelsea develop the love, acceptance, and faith needed to find their happily ever after?

Fourth and Long: A Three Rivers Ranch Romance (Book 3): Commander Brett Murphy goes to Three Rivers Ranch to find some rest and relaxation with his Army buddies. Having his ex-wife show up with a seven-year-old she claims is his son is anything but the R&R he craves. Kate needs to make amends, and Brett needs to find forgiveness, but are they too late to find their happily ever after?

Fifth Generation Cowboy: A Three Rivers Ranch Romance (Book 4): Tom Lovell has watched his friends find their true happiness on Three Rivers Ranch, but everywhere he looks, he only sees friends. Rose Reyes has been bringing her daughter out to the ranch for equine therapy for months, but it doesn't seem to be working. Her challenges with Mari are just as frustrating as ever. Could Tom be exactly what Rose needs? Can he remove his friendship blinders and find love with someone who's been right in front of him all this time?

Sixth Street Love Affair: A Three Rivers Ranch Romance (Book 5): After losing his wife a few years back, Garth Ahlstrom thinks he's ready for a second chance at love. But Juliette Thompson has a secret that could destroy their budding relationship. Can they find the strength, patience, and faith to make things work?

The Seventh Sergeant: A Three Rivers Ranch Romance (Book 6): Life has finally started to settle down for Sergeant Reese Sanders after his devastating injury overseas. Discharged from the Army and now with a good job at Courage Reins, he's finally found happiness—until a horrific fall puts him right back where he was years ago: Injured and depressed. Carly Watters, Reese's new veteran care coordinator, dislikes small towns almost as much as she loathes cowboys. But she finds herself faced with both when she gets assigned to Reese's case. Do they have the humility and faith to make their relationship more than professional?

Eight Second Ride: A Three Rivers Ranch Romance (Book 7): Ethan Greene loves his work at Three Rivers Ranch, but he can't seem to find the right woman to settle down with. When sassy yet vulnerable Brynn Bowman shows up at the ranch to recruit him back to the rodeo circuit, he takes a different approach with the barrel racing champion. His patience and newfound faith pay off when a friendship--and more--starts with Brynn. But she wants out of the rodeo circuit right when Ethan wants to rejoin. Can they find the path God wants them to take and still stay together?

The First Lady of Three Rivers Ranch: A Three Rivers Ranch Romance (Book 8): Heidi Duffin has been dreaming about opening her own bakery since she was thirteen years old. She scrimped and saved for years to afford baking and pastry school in San Francisco. And now she only has one year left before she's a certified pastry chef. Frank Ackerman's father has recently retired, and he's taken over the largest cattle ranch in the Texas Panhandle. A horseman through and through, he's also nearing thirty-one and looking for someone to bring love and joy to a homestead that's been dominated by men for a decade. But when he convinces Heidi to come clean the cowboy cabins, she changes all that. But the siren's call of a bakery is still loud in Heidi's ears, even if she's also seeing a future with Frank. Can she rely on her faith in ways she's never had to before or will their relationship end when summer does?

Christmas in Three Rivers: A Three Rivers Ranch Romance (Book 9): Isn't Christmas the best time to fall in love? The cowboys of Three Rivers Ranch think so. Join four of them as they journey toward their path to happily ever after in four, all-new novellas in the Amazon #1 Bestselling Three Rivers Ranch Romance series.

THE NINTH INNING: The Christmas season has never felt like such a burden to boutique owner Andrea Larsen. But with Mama gone and the holidays upon her, Andy finds herself wishing she hadn't been so quick to judge her former boyfriend, cowboy Lawrence Collins. Well, Lawrence hasn't forgotten about Andy either, and he devises a plan to get her out to the ranch so they can reconnect. Do they have the faith and humility to patch things up and start a new relationship?

TEN DAYS IN TOWN: Sandy Keller is tired of the dating scene in Three Rivers. Though she owns the pancake house, she's looking for a fresh start, which means an escape from the town where she grew up. When her older brother's best friend, Tad Jorgensen, comes to town for the holidays, it is a balm to his weary soul. A helicopter tour guide who experienced a near-death experience, he's looking to start over too--but in Three Rivers. Can Sandy and Tad navigate their troubles to find the path God wants them to take--and discover true love--in only ten days?

ELEVEN YEAR REUNION: Pastry chef extraordinaire, Grace Lewis has moved to Three Rivers to help Heidi Ackerman open a bakery in Three Rivers. Grace relishes the idea of starting over in a town where no one knows about her failed cupcakery. She doesn't expect to run into her old high school boyfriend, Jonathan Carver. A carpenter working at Three Rivers Ranch, Jon's in town against his will. But with Grace now on the scene, Jon's thinking life in Three Rivers is suddenly looking up. But with her focus on baking and his disdain for small towns, can they make their eleven year reunion stick?

THE TWELFTH TOWN: Newscaster Taryn Tucker has had enough of life on-screen. She's bounced from town to town before arriving in Three Rivers, completely alone and completely anonymous--just the way she now likes it. She takes a job cleaning at Three Rivers Ranch, hoping for a chance to figure out who she is and where God wants her. When she meets happy-go-lucky cowhand Kenny Stockton, she doesn't expect sparks to fly. Kenny's always been "the best friend" for his female friends, but the pull between him and Taryn can't be denied. Will they have the courage and faith necessary to make their opposite worlds mesh?

Lucky Number Thirteen: A Three Rivers Ranch Romance (Book 10): Tanner Wolf, a rodeo champion ten times over, is excited to be riding in Three Rivers for the first time since he left his philandering ways and found religion. Seeing his old friends Ethan and Brynn is therapuetic--until a terrible accident lands him in the hospital. With his rodeo career over, Tanner thinks maybe he'll stay in town--and it's not just because his nurse, Summer Hamblin, is the prettiest woman he's ever met. But Summer's the queen of first dates, and as she looks for a way to make a relationship with the transient rodeo star work Summer's not sure she has the fortitude to go on a second date. Can they find love among the tragedy?

The Curse of February Fourteenth: A Three Rivers Ranch Romance (Book 11): Cal Hodgkins, cowboy veterinarian at Bowman's Breeds, isn't planning to meet anyone at the masked dance in small-town Three Rivers. He just wants to get his bachelor friends off his back and sit on the sidelines to drink his punch. But when he sees a woman dressed in gorgeous butterfly wings and cowgirl boots with blue stitching, he's smitten. Too bad she runs away from the dance before he can get her name, leaving only her boot behind...

Fifteen Minutes of Fame: A Three Rivers Ranch Romance (Book 12): Navy Richards is thirty-five years of tired—tired of dating the same men, working a demanding job, and getting her heart broken over and over again. Her aunt has always spoken highly of the matchmaker in Three Rivers, Texas, so she takes a six-month sabbatical from her high-stress job as a pediatric nurse, hops on a bus, and meets with the matchmaker. Then she meets Gavin Redd. He's handsome, he's hardworking, and he's a cowboy. But is he an Aquarius too? Navy's not making a move until she knows for sure...

Sixteen Steps to Fall in Love: A Three Rivers Ranch Romance (Book 13): A chance encounter at a dog park sheds new light on the tall, talented Boone that Nicole can't ignore. As they get to know each other better and start to dig into each other's past, Nicole is the one who wants to run. This time from her growing admiration and attachment to Boone. From her aging parents. From herself.

But Boone feels the attraction between them too, and he decides he's tired of running and ready to make Three Rivers his permanent home. **Can Boone and Nicole use their faith to overcome their differences and find a happily-ever-after together?**

The Sleigh on Seventeenth Street: A Three Rivers Ranch Romance (Book 14): A cowboy with skills as an electrician tries a relationship with a down-on-her luck plumber. Can Dylan and Camila make water and electricity play nicely together this Christmas season? Or will they get shocked as they try to make their relationship work?

ABOUT LIZ

Liz Isaacson writes inspirational romance, usually set in Texas, or Montana, or anywhere else horses and cowboys exist. She lives in Utah, where she teaches elementary school, taxis her daughter to dance several times a week, and eats a lot of Ferrero Rocher while writing. Find her on her website at lizisaacson.com.